ALSO BY NINA LEVINE

Storm MC Series
Storm
Fierce
Blaze
Revive
Slay
Sassy Christmas
Illusive
Command
Havoc

Sydney Storm MC Series
Relent
Nitro's Torment

Crave Series
All Your Reasons
Be The One

Standalone Novels
Steal My Breath
Her Kind of Crazy

RELENT

SYDNEY STORM MC | BOOK 1

USA TODAY BESTSELLING AUTHOR

NINA LEVINE

Editing by Karen Louise Rohde Faergemann at The Word Wench Editing Services
Cover Design ©2015 by Romantic Book Affair Designs
Cover Photography by Wander Aguiar
Cover Model: Dylan Horsch

To everyone who struggles with self-doubt.

YOU ARE ENOUGH.

NEVER DOUBT THAT.

Prologue

Evie – 16 years old

"You do know the only reason every guy in school wants you is because they all think you're just as much of a slut as your mother is, don't you?"

I finished washing my hands before turning off the tap and lifting my head to look in the mirror at the three bitches standing behind me. They always seemed to wait until I was alone in the school toilets before attacking me with their hateful words.

"You do know the reason every guy in school *doesn't* want you is because you're a nasty, spiteful cow, don't you?" I threw back at Stephanie, the ringleader, before turning to face them.

I watched her eyes widen in surprise. She quickly regrouped and spat some more nastiness at me, "You might be pretty now but looks don't last, so I recommend if you actually want to lose that virginity you're hanging onto, to pick one of them and get it done. The rest of your life will be downhill from here and you might not get another chance. I mean, it's gone to shit now anyway, Evie, so I'm not sure why you would even hope that it'll get better. Your sister is gone and your mother screwed her way to fucking up your family . . . and if you think Kick will ever see you as more than a friend, you're dreaming."

My hand connected with her cheek a second later and the sound of the slap echoed through the tiny room. Anger pumped furiously through my veins at her words. She'd been throwing words like these at me for months now and, in my grief, I'd been ignoring them. Ignoring *her*. But she'd pushed me now and I'd had enough.

"Don't you *ever* mention Shelly again!" I yelled, as I desperately tried to fight off the guilt and shame that bubbled up whenever my sister and mother were mentioned.

Will it ever end?

Pain pounded in my head as a headache set in. The headaches were never ending these days, and I knew this one, like all the others, wouldn't ease up for at least the rest of today.

Stephanie stared hate at me as she held her face where I'd slapped her. "Just stay away from Todd and I won't ever mention her again. He's mine and I'm not gonna lose him to a whore like you."

I stood stunned as the three of them gave me one last venomous look before leaving me alone. What the hell? I wasn't even interested in her boyfriend. Slumping against the sink behind me, I ran through all my interactions with Todd lately, trying to work out what she was referring to. Lost in my thoughts, I was caught off guard when the door pushed open and Kick barged in to the room, concern etched on his face.

His eyes found mine and he asked, "Are you alright?"

I rubbed my temples as the headache intensified. "Yeah, why? And why are you barging into the girls' toilets?"

He came toward me, the concern on his face shifting to something else. Frustration. I knew that look from him well. "I saw those bitches leaving and Stephanie said something about you being in here and needing me." He paused and came even closer, his eyes now demanding honesty from me. "I know you're not okay, Evie. When are you gonna admit it and ask for help?"

Always my protector. But this time you can't save me.

The pain throbbed harder in my head and I struggled for

2

breath.

I can't do this now.

I wrapped my arms around myself, my fingers clawing at my arms, digging into my skin. Desperately wanting to force the despair and hopelessness out of me.

"Don't you see, Kick? Even if I ask for help, there's nothing you can do. Not this time." He'd always been there for me, helping me pick up the pieces when they smashed around me. I knew he thought he could fix me, fix this horrible situation, but it was time *he* admitted it – no one could fix this.

He listened to what I said, his body tensing as he processed it all. Anger tore across his face and I gripped the sink as I waited for his explosion. Kick had a temper and it was about to unleash itself. Although he was only seventeen, I'd seen grown men shrink under his temper.

"Fuck!" he roared, turning around and punching the door. I remained silent and simply watched as he punched it again, his back muscles rippling under his tight t-shirt. Stephanie had been right when she'd said I wanted Kick to see me as more than a friend. But even I knew that would never happen. Although he was single now, he usually had a girlfriend or a girl he was sleeping with. He was my best friend and that was all it would ever be. And I'd made peace with that a long time ago. But it didn't stop me admiring everything Kick was.

Good-looking with olive skin, brown hair that begged for fingers to be run through it, green eyes I could get lost in for days, and built with muscles gained from hours of football training.

He turned back to face me and scrubbed his hand over his face. "I'm gonna go and sort that bitch out for you once and for all. I've had enough of watching them tear you down for something that wasn't your fault."

3

We stared at each other for a couple more moments before he stalked out of the toilets.

Shit.

I had to stop him before he went too far.

I had to make him see.

This *was* my fault.

I deserved everything I got.

Chapter One

Evie

I'd hit it.

That moment in life when you grow weary of trying.

When you've taken so many steps forward and twice as many back and you throw your hands in the air and say to fuck with it.

I was done.

Done caring.

Done wanting to care.

Done with it all.

Life could try and drag me back into the game all it liked, but I was out.

As I sat in the afternoon traffic with tears streaming down my face, I kept my hands firmly on the steering wheel and let them fall. Jeremy was always telling me to let it all hang out, to not hide myself from the world, so I was only honouring him by not giving a shit how bad I looked. And yet, as we sat bumper to bumper, not moving, I was sure the driver in the next car must have been looking at me, judging me. I glanced in his direction to find him engrossed with his phone. I stared for a couple of minutes but he never gave me the time of day.

Nobody cares, Evie.

Not me, not him, and not the driver that killed Jeremy.

I sagged against the steering wheel as the pain sliced through me.

Again.

It had been nearly a week and the pain was as intense as it had been the day he died. But I knew from experience the pain would never go away. Eventually, I'd numb myself to it, but still, I'd carry it with me to my grave. Jeremy and I were entwined so deeply that some days I hadn't known where he ended and I began. We'd been a part of each other's lives since we were ten.

Since Kick brought him home from school and declared him a part of us now.

Shit.

And that was the kicker.

Now I'd lost both of them.

***

It took me twice as long to get home from work than usual due to the horrendous traffic. As I pulled into my driveway, I saw my best friend, Maree, sitting on my front step. She hadn't left me alone since Jeremy's death, and I was at the point where I needed some space. I loved her dearly but she never knew when to back off.

Sighing, I grabbed my bag from the passenger seat and gave myself a quick onceover in the mirror. Shit, I looked awful. My mascara wasn't waterproof after all, and I had black streaks running down my face. Add to that, my foundation had worn off in the heat of the day and my long, brunette hair had frizzed in the humidity, and I looked like a woman you would possibly cross the road to avoid.

Maree came towards me as I stepped out of the car. "You look like you need a girl's night in," she said, assessing me.

Maree was the kind of woman who never stepped foot outside her house unless she was immaculately presented. Even after a long day at her teaching job, with teenagers harassing her, she still looked good. Makeup still perfect, blonde hair swept up into a ponytail, black dress almost wrinkle free and heels not even affecting her feet. "I hate you, Maree," I muttered, taking it all in.

She raised a perfect eyebrow. "Why?"

"Because you always look good and it's not fair," I answered as I walked past her to the front door of my house.

She followed close behind me. "Evie, have you taken a look in the mirror lately? You could wear a goddamn sack and look hot. Without even doing your hair or makeup. I have to spend hours in front of the mirror to achieve what you wake up with."

I turned to look at her and frowned. "What I wake up with? Bed head and a puffy face?"

Shaking her head, she said, "No, sex appeal. You can't fake that shit, and you were lucky to be born with it. Even standing here with your messy hair, non-existent makeup, and fucking mascara all over your face, you still look sexy. Any guy would pick you over me any day."

She was wrong, but I didn't have the energy to argue. Besides, I hadn't been laid in six months so I didn't know where all these men were who she thought would be interested in me. "I still hate you," I said, and resumed my journey to the front door. My thoughts had shifted now to how I was going to break it to her that I needed a night off rather than a girl's night in. Maree wasn't one to give up easily when she was on a mission. And her mission at the moment was to get me through my grief. What she didn't seem to understand was that time spent with her wasn't going to take away my sadness.

As I unlocked the door and entered my house, I could hear her rambling on about her day. Her words drifted in and out as I trudged down my long hall to the kitchen at the back of the

7

house. I caught snippets of 'those kids will be the death of me' and 'it's only February and I already need a holiday'. But mostly, I was lost in a fog where her words floated in my mind alongside images of Jeremy. Laughing, being a dickhead, dancing…all the fun we'd had over the years had replayed over and over in my mind this week. Like a movie. A movie I couldn't switch off.

"Evie! Are you listening to me?"

Her shrill tone snapped me back to the moment. "What?"

She dumped her bag on my cluttered kitchen counter, and my attention drifted to the mess. I never let my house go like this, but this week I just couldn't have given a shit about it, and it showed. Dishes were piled next to the sink, unopened mail lay scattered on the counter, and other junk had accumulated that I didn't have the energy to sort out.

"Evie!"

I blinked and gave my attention back to her. Pulling out a seat at the kitchen table, I sighed and collapsed onto it. Looking up at her, I said, "Sorry, I'm not with it this afternoon."

I'm with Jeremy.

I wish I was with Jeremy.

She sat with me, her face full of sympathy and concern. "I know, but you need to get yourself together because the funeral is tomorrow."

All of the grief and anger I had churning in me spewed out and I was helpless to stop it. "I don't have to get myself together, Maree. Fuck that. I'll go to the damn funeral but I'm only doing that for Jeremy, and he wouldn't have given a shit if I was the crazy lady at the funeral who howled her way through it and let her fucking mascara drip all over the seat. In fact, he'd *want* me to be the crazy lady. He was always telling me to let myself go and just feel. Well, fuck it, after all this time, I'm not

8

going to give a fuck about appearances. I'm going to feel it all, and if anyone doesn't like the way I deal, they can go screw themselves."

Her eyes widened, clearly surprised at my outburst, but she gave me a big smile. "Well, okay then! I'm liking this new Evie." She reached into her bag and pulled out a packet of facial cleansing wipes. Maree kept a full kit of makeup on her at all times. Passing a wipe to me, she said, "Here, clean off your mascara, babe."

My face was the least of my worries, but I took it from her and did as she said. "I'll be okay on my own tonight."

She frowned. "I don't want to leave you on your own."

"Maree, I'm going to get through this. It'll take some time, but just because I'm a mess doesn't mean I can't be on my own." I paused and then added softly, "I *need* to be on my own tonight."

Her lips pursed together. I knew this was going to be a battle. Maree was the kind of person who always needed to be surrounded by people whereas I didn't. I craved time to myself and felt like I would go crazy when I didn't get enough of it. "I really don't think that's a good idea, Evie. I don't mind hanging out with you if that's what you're worried about."

My weariness intensified. I just wanted her to go so I could have a shower and then curl up in my bed and wallow in my grief. She wasn't making it easy for me, though, and even the thought of having to argue with her over it heightened my exhaustion. "No, that's not what I'm worried about. You know me, and you know I like time to myself. That's all this is about. I know that you think you know better about what I need, but just because it's what *you* would want if you were me doesn't mean it's what *I* want. Can you understand that?"

Hurt flickered across her face but she covered it well and nodded. "Okay," she whispered and pushed her chair back to stand. Looking down at me, she said, "But if you need me, all you have to do is call."

As relief filled me that she'd listened, I reached for her hand and squeezed it. "Thank you. You're a good friend."

She slung her bag over her shoulder and gave me one last smile. "I'm always here for you, Evie. I just wish I could take away all the bad shit for you."

I gave her a weak smile and nodded. "I know, babe. I know."

When the front door closed shut a couple of moments later, I took a deep breath and then pushed it back out. My heart sat heavy in my chest. Over the years, so many people had stomped on it, but this felt the worst.

Maybe it had finally taken one too many beatings.

Maybe the patches I'd given it were no longer enough to hold it together.

Maybe it needed more than bandages to put it back together.

And if that was the case, I was screwed.

Love had packed up and walked out of my life a long time ago.

Chapter Two

Kick

"You ready to fuck some assholes up?" King asked me as he passed me a beer.

I took the drink and drank some before asking him, "Who?"

He shifted forward in his seat to speak which was a good thing. Even though it was only eleven in the morning, it was busy in the clubhouse bar, and the noise, combined with the deafness in my left ear, made it hard for me to hear what he was saying.

"Someone who fucked with someone I love. And whoever is with him when we get to him." He took a swig of his beer and sat patiently waiting for my answer.

I didn't ask him any further questions. I never did. When King had a job for me, I did it without hesitation. Looking at my President now, I thought back to the first day I'd met him. Thirteen years ago. I'd been twenty-two and he'd only been a couple of years older, but, even back then, he'd been a law unto himself. He wasn't our President at the time, but all the boys knew he'd be the next one.

"You in on this or do you want me to go alone?" I asked.

He grinned his wicked fucking grin that told me he wouldn't miss this for the world. King was a bloodthirsty motherfucker and liked to be hands-on whenever he could. "I'm in and we do this tonight. Meet me at the clubhouse at midnight."

I nodded and silently drank more of my beer. Drinking with King was easy. He was a man of few words – one of his best traits as far as I was concerned. I'd never had a problem or disagreement with him, unlike a lot of the club members. He was a hard man and expected a lot, but if you kept your head down and got the shit done he needed you to, then you were all good. King and I were good.

After a couple of silent moments, he said, "Heard you were heading out to a funeral today. Were you close to him?"

Regret punched me in the gut.

Was I close to him?

I should have been fucking closer and that shit was on me, not Jeremy.

It was *my* fault that, when he'd died, he hadn't known how fucking sorry I was that we'd spent the last five years not having each other's backs. "Yeah, brother. We grew up together and he helped me through a lot of shit. But we kinda lost track of each other for a while there. Only just got back in touch three months ago."

"Fuck," he muttered. The emotion that momentarily crossed his face was more than I'd seen on it in months. That surprised the hell out of me; the only emotions King tended to exhibit were anger or a manic-like excitement. King wasn't full of deep emotions. Well, not that I'd ever seen.

"He died in a car accident. Drunk driver took him out."

"Motherfucker," he snarled as he abruptly stood up. Looking down at me with a feral look, he said, "You find the cunt that did it, bring that name to me, and I will make fucking sure he never does it again."

I stared up at him, unsure where his sudden outburst had come from, and simply nodded.

He leant his hand on the table and dipped his head towards mine. "We clear, Kick? I want that fucking name."

"We're clear."

12

Straightening, he gave me one last hard nod before stalking out of the room. He ran into our

Vice President, Hyde, on the way, and after they had a quick conversation, Hyde made his way to me. I eyed him, uncertain about his mood today, and waited for him to speak so I could gauge where he was at.

With a jerk of his chin, he said, "King says you're at a funeral for the rest of the day."

"Yeah. Why? Have you got something you need me to take care of?"

"See, that's why I fuckin' like you, Kick. And it's why you're mine and King's go-to-guy when shit needs to be done. Can't fuckin' count on anyone the way we can on you."

"What time do you need me back here?" I asked him.

"Four. That work for you?"

"Yeah, I can do that."

"Good." And with that, he turned and left.

I watched him as he barked something at one of the other guys. *Jekyll and Hyde.* That was our VP. Never could be sure if he would rip your head off or buy you a drink. I'd had a few run-ins with him, but the thing about Hyde was unless you really screwed him over, he didn't tend to hold onto shit. Unlike King who remembered every little fucking thing done to him and always made sure payback was delivered at some point.

As Hyde exited the room, I emptied my glass and stood. It was time to visit old ghosts.

And old flames.

***

"Evie," I called out as I jogged to catch up to her, the heat of the day causing my shirt to stick to me.

13

She stopped and turned to face me, her body language clear. She didn't want to talk to me. Sighing, she murmured, "What do you want, Kick?"

Fuck.

Beauty like I'd seen on no other woman lit her face, even today when I knew she would be struggling with what we'd just sat through. The tiredness I saw on her face was a dead giveaway to her grief, as were her unruly hair and lack of makeup. I'd spent most of the funeral watching her, taking in the changes to her body since I'd last seen her just over a year ago. The curves I'd grown up loving had almost disappeared. The black dress she wore today hung limply off her whereas in the past, it would have hugged the shit out of her. Evie had always had hang-ups about her body but I'd always fucking loved it. The more curves the better as far as I was concerned.

I let my eyes wander over her. Even in her curve-less and exhausted state, she turned me on. I was sure she always would. "Are you okay?" I asked, silently willing her to speak to me rather than pushing me away like I knew she probably wanted to do.

Her mask slipped for a moment and then she quickly put it back in place before saying, "I'll be fine."

I took a step closer to her and as she tried to move away from me, I quickly flicked my hand out and caught her wrist, halting her movement. "Don't do that," I said, annoyed we were back here, back to a place where she tried to hide herself from me.

"Do what?"

"That thing you do where you shut down and sweep your feelings away as if they don't matter." She'd been doing it for as long as I'd known her. Twenty-seven years. "You lost a friend, Evie . . . *we* lost a friend, and I'm sure as fuck not coping with it so I know you've gotta be struggling too."

14

She pulled free of my hold. "He's gone, and we've gotta keep going. Simple as that."

What the fuck?

"You're fuckin' kidding me, right?" I asked, my voice hard. Forceful. Demanding. Her words made no sense. Jeremy had been like family to us growing up, and there was no way we just moved on from this. No way *she* would just move on from this.

"No, I'm not. Funerals are to say goodbye, and I've just said goodbye." Her brown eyes betrayed her, though. She was struggling with this, too.

"That's bullshit. It's gonna take us a long time to say goodbye. That shit isn't covered in a fuckin' funeral, Evie."

Those brown eyes of hers flared with what I figured was anger. "How would you know how long it'll take me? You haven't seen me in a year, Kick, so you have no idea what's going on with me anymore. Don't come back here today thinking you know me, 'cause you *don't*. The day you walked out on me three years ago was the day I changed." She was angry, and yet her voice held none of the angry passion it had when we were together.

I stepped into her space again and bent my face to hers. "I *do* know you. I know how you like to handle shit you don't want to deal with. I know you prefer to shut down and not let your feelings out. And I fuckin' know you feel every-fuckin'-thing deep, babe. Losing Jeremy would have cut you deep and you can try and hide it from everyone, but you can't hide shit from me." I moved my face even closer to hers before I whispered, "I see you, Evie. I've *always* seen you, and I know you're struggling. Let me in."

She froze and stared at me in silence for a beat. Then her breathing picked up as the words fell out of her mouth. "Why now, Kick? Why couldn't you have just come back for the

15

funeral and left me alone?"

The desperate plea in her voice did not go unheard. It was the same fucking question I was asking myself even as I was asking her to let me in.

Why the fuck now?

I didn't answer her, and she demanded again, "Why?"

The anger in her tone fired me up. "You weren't the only one disappointed we ended things three years ago. Did you ever stop to think about that?" I threw my words at her, instantly regretting the harshness of them and wishing like fuck I could scrub them away and start again.

"No, because *you* were the one who ended it!"

And there was the passion that had been missing before. I fucking loved her passion so even though she was mad at me now, I was on cloud-fucking-nine.

She still loves me.

I couldn't hide it, I grinned. And that pissed her off even more. Story of my fucking life.

"What the fuck, Kick?" she snapped. We were still in each other's faces and that fact didn't elude me. She hadn't moved away from me.

We can still make this work.

"I didn't end it, baby. You ended it. Did you forget that?" I said softly.

Confusion flashed across her face and she frowned. I knew her so well it was like I could see her brain flicking through the memories. "I remember we fought and you said you didn't want me in your world."

"Yeah, and then you said you were done and we were done. *You* ended it."

"No! You did. You didn't want me!"

Fuck, I'd missed this. Evie arguing with me turned me way

16

the fuck on. Any other woman yelling at me like this would piss me right off, but not Evie. "I didn't want to bring you into my world. You knew that."

"Jesus, I was already *in* your world. I fucking grew up in your world."

I shook my head. "You know that's not the world I'm talking about - "

She cut me off. "I don't even know why we're arguing over this! It's in the past, and it's done." Her wild eyes stared at me and her shoulders tensed up. Hell, her whole body was tense, and that made my day.

Evie wasn't done with this.

If she were, she wouldn't be lashing out like this.

I raised my brows. "You sure about that?"

She hesitated, and although she tried to act like she hadn't, I caught it. "Yes," she said with determination, but I knew it was more to convince herself than me. Half the time, I knew Evie's next thought and move before her. After being the one she'd confided all her fears, worries and happiness in while growing up, I fucking *knew* how her mind worked.

Again, I shook my head. "No, you're not, and I'm going to show you just how fuckin' unsure of it you really are."

Her eyes widened and she finally moved away from me. I'd expected her to put distance between us from the beginning of the conversation. The fact she hadn't was just another sign she wasn't done with this. When she spoke, it was like all the passion of a minute ago had been drained from her. Exhaustion had stepped back in. "Just leave it, Kick. We tried twice and we couldn't make it work. And we've both changed. We're not those kids who loved each other anymore."

She didn't give me time to say anything else before turning and walking away from me. My mouth opened to call out to her again but I quickly snapped it shut. I'd catch up with her later. I had no intention of letting her walk away from me permanently again, and perhaps I needed to take this slowly. Fuck, I wasn't known for slow, but for Evie I would do anything.

And she was wrong.

We'd always be those kids who loved each other.

Underneath all the shit that was me today, I still loved her.

It was fucked up, though, that it had taken Jeremy's death for me to admit that.

***

Darkness blanketed the clubhouse when I arrived back there at midnight to meet up with King. It was one of the club member's birthdays, so most of the boys were out celebrating with him.

King stood leaning against his bike waiting for me, a grin stretched across his face. I pulled up next to him and waited for his instructions.

"Did you and Hyde get that job done this afternoon?" he asked.

"Yeah, the debt was settled. And it was clean." We'd collected off one of our junkie customers who hadn't paid in over a month. Surprisingly, no blood had been shed.

He nodded. "Good. Now, you ready for some fun?" he asked, a dangerous tone to his voice. I knew what 'fun' meant to King.

With a nod of my head, I said, "You lead the way."

No other words were exchanged and his bike roared to life.

Our destination was fairly close, only about a fifteen-minute ride. When we pulled up outside the run down house with two bikes outside, my gut seized with a mixture of anticipation and concern. King was known for pulling some crazy shit in his time, but to fuck with fellow bikers was a little past crazy.

"What's going on, King?" I asked as I walked towards him.

"One of these fuckers stole off my sister. Payback's gonna be a bitch."

I narrowed my eyes. "And?"

"And what?"

"I'm sensing there's some other shit going on here. Don't fuck with me, brother, tell me the full story so I know what the fuck I'm walking into."

He lit a smoke and took a long drag. When his gaze hit mine, the grin from earlier was gone from his eyes and a hard look had replaced it. "You've got a sister, right?" He waited for my nod and once I gave it, he continued. "My sister is a lot younger than me, twenty-three, and one of these cunts was dating her and thought he'd share her around with his mates at a party when she was drunk. Lucky for her, a friend of mine was there and stepped in. The cunt fucked off and she didn't hear from him again until three days later when he showed up at her house and beat her up and stole the money she'd been saving."

"Fuck," I muttered, understanding his reason for being here now. I'd be here, too, if it was my sister.

"Yeah, fuck. Skylar didn't fucking tell me she was dating him because if she had, I would have put a fucking stop to it. The fucker is a Silver Hell member. I only found all this shit out when my friend called me to ask how she was."

Fuck.

If what I figured was about to go down did actually go down, we were about to declare war with the Silver Hell MC.

King finished his smoke and stubbed it out. Slapping me on the back, he asked, "You with me, brother?"

I never hesitated when it came to my President. "Yeah, I've

19

always got your back."

His eyes lit with that dangerous gleam again. "Let's go party then."

He strode to the front door and banged it hard with the palm of his hand and yelled out, "Open up, motherfucker!"

We waited for less than a minute before the door was yanked open. A pissed-off Silver Hell member glared at us, but only for a second, because King stepped inside the house and sucker punched him. The guy dropped to the ground, knocked out cold, and King stepped over his body to walk down the hallway.

I entered the house and the stench of cigarette smoke, booze and sex hit me. Fuck, I hoped the women had left already. King was unpredictable, yes, but my guess was he wouldn't leave any witnesses alive to tell the tale.

The hallway led into a filthy kitchen full of dirty dishes and rubbish strewn across the counters. It was empty so we continued into the living room. Still empty in there, but a bloodcurdling scream from an adjoining room alerted us where to go next. King picked up the pace and kicked the door in without even attempting to open it. Jacked up on adrenaline and a desire for revenge, nothing would stop him now.

"What the fuck is going on here?" King thundered as he came to a halt the minute he entered the room.

I followed him in and stopped, too, sickened at the sight in front of us. A Silver Hell's biker had a naked girl strapped to the bed, spreadeagled. He sat atop her but I could see her face, and she didn't look to be any older than about sixteen. And it wasn't consent written across her stricken face.

"Fuck," I muttered. I'd seen a lot of shit in my life, but this type took the fucking cake. The fact the guy was still fully clothed gave me hope that he hadn't done too much to her yet. Regardless, this shit was fucked up.

The guy shifted off the bed and came towards us, a menacing glare in his eyes. "What the fuck business is it of yours, and how the fuck did you get in here?" He was tall and built, and his body was tensed, ready for a fight. He'd obviously never met my president; I'd never known King to lose a fight.

"The name Skylar ring a fucking bell, asshole?" King demanded.

A look of recognition crossed the guy's face but he said, "Never heard that name in my life. Now fuck off and leave me the hell alone."

King seethed with anger, the rage clinging to his words as he said, "Your first mistake, Marco, was fucking with my sister. Your second mistake was raping the girl on your bed, and your last fucking mistake will be lying to me."

He stepped towards Marco and punched him hard in the face. The sound of bone cracking vibrated around the room. The guy retaliated, aiming a punch at King's cheek, but King blocked it, shoving the guy backwards and into the wall. As he sagged against it, and slid to the ground, King advanced and stood over him.

"Wanna tell me the truth now?" he asked, his voice deathly calm and controlled.

Marco glared up at him and then spat at his feet. "Your sister was a good fucking root, man. That cunt of hers was sweet and tight -"

King cut him off with a punch to the jaw. His head swung to the side and hit the bedside table before King hauled him up by his shirt, swung him around and shoved him forcefully into the other wall. It was obvious from the look on King's face that he had only one thing on his mind – death.

As King continued to rain pain down onto the guy, I turned my attention to the girl on the bed. Terror flashed in her eyes and as I walked towards her, her whole body flinched as if she was trying desperately to escape me.

I shook my head. "You're safe with me, darlin'," I murmured as I pulled my knife from its sheath. Cutting the ropes tied to her wrists and feet, I freed her. She scrambled into a huddled position with her knees up and arms around them, and stared at me in silence, obviously waiting to see what I would do to her.

Fuck, I hated this shit. Hated the fear she felt because of a man who believed it was his right to take whatever he wanted from a woman.

I sat on the bed beside her and pointed at King who was still beating the shit out of the rapist asshole. "That man's sister was used by the guy who was raping you, and that's why we're here. He won't stop until he kills the guy, at which point we'll take you wherever you want to go. You're safe with us. Okay?"

Her eyes widened and then she nodded. "Thank you," she whispered, her body visibly relaxing a little.

"Good. Now where are your clothes?"

She jerked her chin towards the corner of the room and I located them and brought them to her. "Get dressed, 'cause I don't think we're gonna be here much longer," I said as I took in the bloodied mess King was creating.

I left her to it and walked back to where King was. "You need a hand, boss?" I asked.

He stopped mid-punch and looked up at me. His long dark hair stuck to his sweaty face, his eyes held the crazy that I knew he was made of, and his breaths were coming hard. "Does it look like I need a fucking hand, smartass?" he asked. He'd knocked Marco unconscious and, by the looks of it, Marco's remaining breaths were limited.

I grinned and shrugged. "Just making sure, old man. I mean,

22

you're nearing forty so I figure your body might start letting you down soon."

"Fuck off," he muttered, and went back to what he was doing.

I waited in silence. The only sounds in the room were of fists colliding with bones and the grunts King made as he took his revenge. I'd lost count of the number of times this scenario had played out over the last thirteen years. King liked to take back-up when he went on one of his missions, but he rarely needed it.

The sound of whimpering caught my attention and I turned to the girl. She stood by the bed staring at King, tears streaming down her face. My natural instinct was to go to her and wrap her in my arms; however, I figured after being attacked by one stranger, she'd hardly want another stranger touching her. Instead, I said to King, "Can we hurry this the fuck up, 'cause we've got a woman we need to get out of here."

King straightened, took a step away from the body lying at his feet, and turned to me. Blood covered his shirt, some of his face and his hands. He looked like he'd stepped out of a horror movie but it wasn't anything I'd never seen before. His gaze flicked to the girl. "You wanna see me end his life so you know for sure he won't ever hurt you again, or would you prefer to leave the room?"

"Fuck, King, like she needs to see anymore shit," I said, before she could answer him. King had some fucked-up ideas sometimes.

He glared at me. "Let the girl decide. Maybe she'll surprise the fuck out of you."

I returned his glare before turning to her. She stood staring at me in panic, shaking her head at the idea. It looked like she wasn't even taking breaths.

I nodded and started walking to her. It was clear she was

23

about to lose her shit and I needed to get her out of here. When I reached her, I pulled her close to me and said, "It's okay, I'll get you out of here before - "

The shot rang out and her scream tore through me as her eyes looked past me to King.

Fuck.

Motherfucker.

I gripped her harder and levelled an angry stare on King. "What the fuck?" I roared, "She didn't want to fucking see that!"

King's eyes had morphed from wild crazy to deranged crazy. When he spoke, his words dripped with lunacy and the hardness that was signature King. "I don't give a fuck what she thought she wanted. She *needed* to see that."

"No, she fuckin' didn't."

We faced off, glaring at each other. King was amped, his body taut and full of rage. I knew that look from past experience. He hadn't rid himself of the need to exact revenge yet; he still had more in him and he'd have to find a way to work that out of his mind and body before the night was over.

He dismissed me with a wave of his gun. "Get her out of my fucking sight."

She whimpered in my hold, her body wracked with sobs. Without another word to King, I began dragging her out of the room. I moved fast, and when we made it to where the other guy was lying passed out in the hallway, I stepped over his body and roughly pulled the girl outside with me. I knew what King would do with him and she didn't need to see any more death.

I had her on the back of my bike and was just about to leave when another gunshot sounded. A moment later, King stepped outside and stalked to us.

"You take her, and I'll call Bronze," he ordered, still with that deranged glint in his eyes.

24

The cops.

Of course.   Shit was gonna go down between Storm and Silver Hell over this if they ever worked out it was us responsible for the deaths of two members.   King had Bronze on our payroll and it was a smart move to give him a heads-up over this.

As I sped off in the direction the girl gave me, unease slid through me.   The two clubs had existed for years on a mutual agreement to leave each other the fuck alone.   The events of tonight had obliterated that agreement, and while Storm was capable of holding its own, I didn't want to go to battle.

A battle meant death and destruction.

Two things I'd seen enough of to last me a lifetime.

Chapter Three

Evie

I stepped out of the shower, wrapped myself in a towel and walked to the vanity. The woman staring back at me in the mirror seemed more like a stranger than me.

When did I lose myself?

I spread toothpaste onto my toothbrush and tried to avoid my thoughts. They came hard and fast, though, relentlessly chasing me. Trying to force me to face them.

A year ago when you gave up on Kick.

That's when you lost yourself.

Lost your way.

I spat out the toothpaste and rinsed. Slamming the toothbrush down, I muttered, "Shit." I reached for the towel and dried my face. Staring back at myself in the mirror, I traced my finger over the dark bags under my eyes. Leaning closer to the mirror, I stared hard at myself.

Fuck, my grief and exhaustion plastered my face.

Moving my face away from the mirror I reached for my skincare and slathered it on. I still couldn't be bothered with makeup, but at least the skincare might help.

Jeremy's funeral yesterday had taken every last drop of energy from me. And then seeing Kick had sucked anything remaining.

Kick.

Why the hell had he come back? The last year with no

contact had been hard. Harder than the years where we'd been apart but still in touch. At the time, I'd thought those years were hard – having him there but not having him as mine. I'd finally gotten my head together over it all only to have him come and screw with my mind and my heart again.

Just when I'd decided not to care about anything anymore, he'd shown up, and I couldn't get him out of my mind. Turns out I still did care about something. Or rather, someone.

A loud knock on my front door distracted me from my thoughts. Shit, at eight o'clock in the damn morning. Really? They could go to hell, I wasn't ready for visitors.

The knocking turned into loud banging and then I was stunned to hear a female voice I knew well yell out, "Evie, are you home?"

My sister. Who I hadn't spoken to in years.

"Yeah, give me a minute," I yelled back and hurried into my bedroom to put some clothes on.

When I opened the door to her a couple of minutes later, I was surprised to find a woman who hardly resembled my sister staring back at me. Julie had been a thin, well-kept blonde the last time I'd seen her, which was about five years ago. Today, she was overweight, brunette, and had aged more than the five years she actually had.

"Hi," I said, hesitantly. We hadn't parted on the best of terms, and Julie was a bitch at the best of times, so I'd learnt to hedge my bets as to her mood over the years.

She glared at me. "I know you're judging me already so just quit it," she snapped as she pushed past me to stalk down my hall.

I shut the door and turned to follow her. "I see you still haven't learnt to use your filters."

When we reached the kitchen she dumped her bag on the

table and graced me with her glare again. "I just say it as I see it. And you can't tell me you weren't standing there staring at my fat, judging me." She placed her hands on her hips and waited for my reply. Almost as if she was ready for a fight.

"I wasn't judging you, Julie, but I won't deny I noticed it and wondered how you'd gone from where you were to this."

She moved her hands off her hips to hang by her sides, her body easing out of its tense state a little. Only a little, but that was a lot for Julie. "Thank fuck someone can be honest with me."

My tiredness and grief mixed with the absurdity of this whole scenario and caused laughter to bubble up and escape my lips.

She commenced glaring at me again and demanded, "What's so funny?"

I shook my head and threw my hands up in a defensive gesture. "Well, you come to see me, and rather than saying hello and starting a conversation like any normal sister would after all these years, you have a go at me and barge into my house. How screwed up are we? Seriously, it's fucked up, Julie."

She thought about it for a moment and then nodded and gave me a slight smile. "Yeah, I guess it is. But hell, with our family, you can't blame us, right?"

She had a point. "Right." I took a breath and asked, "So why are you here?"

Her whole face softened. I wasn't sure I'd ever seen Julie's face soften like that. "I heard about Jeremy."

My stomach rolled and my breath caught at the mention of his name. I reached out to hold the chair to steady myself.

This is too hard.

I worked to catch my breath again and the nausea passed, but I remained silent. What was there to say, anyway?

"I'm sorry, Evie. I know how much he meant to you."

I met her gaze and found only concern there. She had no ulterior motive for being here which I would have suspected in the past. "Thank you," I said softly and sat at the table.

Julie sat as well and kept talking. "Have you seen Kick?"

"Fuck," I muttered, "do we have to talk about him?"

She shrugged. "Any discussion of you and Jeremy is pointless unless Kick is involved. The three of you were almost joined at the damn hip."

"Jeremy and Kick had a falling-out five years ago, Julie. And Kick and I went our separate ways three years ago, so any inclusion of Kick in this discussion is pointless."

"Shit," she murmured, connecting the dots in her head. "I'd heard you and Kick broke up but I just figured you would have stayed friends like you did the first time you broke up. And I never would have thought Kick and Jeremy would ever stop being friends. What happened?"

I sighed. It seemed I couldn't escape Kick today. "I don't know. Neither of them would tell me."

"And you never pursued that information?"

"I did, but you know those two. Stubborn to the bitter end. Neither would crack, so, in the end, I just let it go."

"That must have been hard. To stay friends with Jeremy while you were with Kick, I mean."

Nodding, I agreed. "Yeah, it was, but I made it work. I did try to make them see sense, but neither would give in." Sadness wrapped me in its arms while I remembered how amazing Jeremy had been throughout that time in my life. He'd never walked away from me, even though it was clear he couldn't be around Kick any longer. And Kick had even managed to not be an asshole about my friendship with Jeremy. It was almost as if the two of them had some agreement about it all but I'd never

29

managed to work it out. I'd just gone with the flow because it had broken my heart that they'd fallen out in the first place. I'd done my best to bring them back together, but that had been a waste of time.

Julie looked at me. *Really* looked at me, as if she was trying to work something out. "Are you going to be okay? I know it's shit right now, but I want to make sure you're coping."

I considered her question, and I also considered her presence here today. "Why today, Julie?"

She knew exactly what I was asking. Sighing, she said, "Let's just say, I've been re-evaluating my life lately. I know we've had our differences in the past, but I'd like to try and put that behind us and spend time together again."

"Why are you suddenly re-evaluating things?" God, I hoped it wasn't sickness or something like that. My body tensed, waiting for her answer.

"I'm a thirty-six-year-old woman with no husband or kids, and I pushed my family away when I was younger and stupid. My best friend recently died from cancer, and I decided life's too short for petty disagreements. So here I am."

The tension relaxed out of my body. "Sorry to hear about your friend, but I'm glad you've decided to make those changes."

"It might take me some time with Mum and Dad, Evie. Don't expect this to just happen overnight. Not after all the shit we've been through."

"I get it." I really did. Our parents were hard work.

"How are they?" she asked tentatively.

I stretched my legs out in front of me and sagged a little in the chair. "They're doing okay at the moment."

"Right, so that means they're still struggling to get their shit together."

She was right. In our family, doing okay didn't mean the same as it would in most families that I knew. "I'll let you decide for yourself once you go and see them."

She stood and picked up her bag. "I've got to get to work. It was good to see you."

I stood as well and moved to hug her. She awkwardly tried to return the hug and that offering spread warmth through me. Julie was not an affectionate person so this hug meant the world to me. When we pulled apart, I smiled at her and said, "Thank you for coming and don't be a stranger. And go and see Mum and Dad."

She nodded and I expected her to say something about them, but she didn't. What she did say took me by surprise. "I don't know what happened between you two, but is there any way for you and Kick to work out your differences? Assuming he's not with someone else now, that is?"

"He's not, but I don't think so. We've been through too much, and if we couldn't make it work the two times we tried, I doubt we could now."

"I don't believe that, Evie. The Kick I remember would do anything for you. *Anything.*"

I wrapped my arms around me. She was wrong, and I needed to protect my heart this time. "I don't think he would. Not anymore," I said softly.

Her face took on that look a person got when they were trying to make you see something their way. "Go through your memories again. Try and remember back to when you were kids. I know he would have done anything for you back then. You two are so connected...between your childhood, our families, Jeremy, the stuff you've both been through...that can't count for nothing, Evie." She paused and stared hard at me before adding on a whisper, "Make it count. You two deserve

31

happiness."

And then she was gone and I was left alone.

Consumed by memories.

***

Evie
16 years old

"Kick! Stop!" I chased after him but he didn't stop. No surprise there. When Kick decided to do something, nothing got in his way.

I rushed after him as he stalked towards the basketball courts where Stephanie and her posse were. His back muscles were tensed, ready for the showdown. Those bitches had been harassing me for months and he'd been itching to take them on, but I would never let him. There was no way I could hold him back now, but really, they deserved whatever he had in mind.

Unless he physically lashed out at them.

That thought sent cold chills through my veins. I was sure he wouldn't lay a hand on a girl, but what if his anger and need to stand up for me made him do something stupid?

I picked up my pace and yelled out to him again. "Kick, please stop! I can handle those bitches myself."

He kept going without a second glance in my direction. The girls spotted him and all turned to face him. The other kids noticed the standoff and they, too, turned to watch. Everyone began closing in on Kick and the girls, and I hated that I had put him in this situation.

He finally made it to them and stopped. I couldn't see his face but I could imagine his glare. That look from Kick was enough to make most people consider their next step but Stephanie didn't cower. She actually took a step closer to him and sent a glare his way.

"Why the fuck can't you bitches leave Evie alone? You don't even

32

know what shit really went down with her family, so you should shut the fuck up rather than spreading nasty gossip and treating her like a slut," he raged. I could tell from his voice how close to the edge he was.

Not good.

"I know her mother cheated on her father and that's a slut as far as I'm concerned. Like mother, like daughter," Stephanie countered.

Kick's arm moved as if he was about to raise it but he kept himself under control and instead clenched his fist over and over, as if he was fighting the urge to punch someone. "I'm not gonna fucking argue this shit with you, Stephanie. Leave Evie alone." His voice had dropped to a menacing tone.

Stephanie said something to him but a hand on my shoulder and the brush past me of a male body distracted me from her.

Jeremy.

"Sorry, Evie," he murmured, as he shoved me aside and kept advancing towards Kick.

I missed what Stephanie said but zeroed back in on Kick who had raised his voice. "You don't wanna start something with me. Trust me on that," he threatened just before Jeremy stepped in.

Jeremy placed his hand on Kick's shoulder. Kick's head jerked around to see who it was but before he could say anything, Jeremy spoke calmly to Stephanie. "Why do you always have to be such a bitch, Stephanie? I'm seriously beginning to wonder about your parents and just what they get up to." He paused, and I saw her face flinch. Jeremy gave Kick a grin and then continued, "Yeah, I think we might look into that, Kick, and then report back what we find."

Stephanie's face contorted into anger like I'd never seen before. "Leave me the fuck alone, Jeremy," she spat before saying to her bitches, "Come on, girls, these three aren't worth our breath." Then she turned and stalked away from us and her posse followed.

I stood there, stunned, not sure what had just happened.

Jeremy slapped Kick on the back and then looked at me with a grin.

33

"All sorted, Evie. That bitch won't give you grief anymore."

I frowned. "How do you know that? And what the hell just happened?"

Kick stopped staring after the girls and turned to look at me. "Jeremy did some digging. Discovered that Stephanie's dad is having an affair at the moment."

"Oh my god! What a two-faced cow to give me shit about my mother."

Jeremy came to me and laid his arm across my shoulders, and pulled me close. "Yeah, thought you might like that."

I looked up at him and smiled. "Thank you."

He jerked his chin at Kick. "Don't thank me, thank him. Kick had the brilliant idea to find out what she was hiding and then to use it against her."

My gaze landed on Kick. He stood still, staring at me with a look I wasn't sure I knew. It gave me goosebumps. "Thank you," I whispered, my stomach doing butterflies, "you're always looking out for me and I've never done anything to deserve it." It was true. For as long as I'd known him, Kick had always stood up for me, and I'd never really given him anything in return or helped him in any way.

He shoved his hands in his pockets and scowled at me. "Don't fucking say shit like that, Evie. You'd do the same thing for me and Jeremy."

Kick didn't usually speak to me like that and it confused me. I stared at him silently, wondering what caused him to do it.

Jeremy punched him in the arm. "Don't be a dick," he muttered.

I watched as the two of them glared at each other for a few moments and then Kick looked at me and said, "Sorry, I'm an asshole. But don't put yourself down, okay? You've been there for me more than you know." His voice cracked a little on his last sentence and he seemed so uncomfortable saying it all. But, at the same time, I could feel the honesty in his words.

34

I smiled at him and then Jeremy broke the moment with another slap on Kick's back. "Okay, let's round this up, guys," he said as he draped his arm around me again. "I've got fucking math homework and I need Evie to work it out for me."

Kick grinned. "She needs to work my shit out, too."

I rolled my eyes. "Are you two ever going to do your own work?"

They stared at me like I was an idiot, and then both their faces broke out in larger grins. "Fuck no," they said in unison as the three of us began walking home.

I laughed.

No matter what I was going through in my life, these two always made my day better.

I hoped I always had them in my life.

***

After Julie left, I headed over to my mother's house. I checked in with her almost daily. Whereas my father usually kept me at arm's length, my mother was the exact opposite - needy.

"Mum, you home?" I yelled out as I unlocked the front door and entered her house. Stupid question really, because aside from going to work, my mother hardly left her home.

"In the kitchen," came her reply.

I kicked off my shoes just inside the front door because Mum had a thing against shoes in the house. As I did this, I noticed the black boots sitting near the door and wondered who they belonged to.

And then I heard a male voice.

Kick.

What the hell? He hardly ever visited my mother.

I hurried to the kitchen and as I rounded the corner, I came

35

face to face with him. I had to grab onto the counter to steady myself so I didn't run into him. My gaze hit his neck and took in the tattoos there before it travelled up to his face, taking in his beard and brown hair that always had that just-fucked look.

His hands grabbed my arms to also help steady me, and my tummy did somersaults at the contact.

It's been too long since he's held me.

"Evie," he murmured, his deep voice awakening the desire I'd always felt for him. The goddamn desire I'd fought hard to rid myself of. But after seeing him at Jeremy's funeral, I knew the desire was as strong as ever.

Fuck.

I tried to move out of his embrace but he wouldn't let me go. I glared at him. "Let me go, Kick."

He held me for another couple of moments before doing as I'd asked. I placed my hands on his chest to try to force him to step aside so I could enter the kitchen, but he didn't move, and all I succeeded in doing was shooting more desire throughout my body at the feel of his body again.

He glanced down at my hands on his chest and then looked at me from under hooded eyes.

Those green eyes.

Damn.

"Feels good, baby," he whispered, his voice thick with unmistakable hunger and those damn eyes penetrating mine, radiating more of that hunger.

My core sang out its need but I acted like I had no clue what he was going on about. I remained silent and tried to push him again. Jesus, his muscles had multiplied since the last time I'd touched him. And they were rock hard. Good lord, I was done for if he pushed this. I could keep my heart closed but my body could never deny him.

He dipped his face towards mine and said, "Your hands on me feels . . . good. Been too fuckin' long."

God, why do you hate me?

Why do you send temptation my way when you know it will only lead to more heartbreak?

I dropped my hands and tried to harden my gaze. I needed to show him I had no intention of going there with him again. "And it won't happen again," I snapped. "Now let me through."

His brows raised but he stepped aside, and I finally entered the kitchen to find my mother busy at the sink washing up. Tupperware containers surrounded her, confusing the hell out of me.

"What's going on?" I asked.

She kept washing but turned her head to look at me. Smiling, she said, "Kick dropped by to say hello and I'm thankful he did because I got him to change the washer on the tap. It had been leaking for ages, driving me crazy."

"You should have asked me to do it, Mum."

She frowned. "You know how to do that?"

Kick chuckled from behind me and muttered, "Yeah she does, 'cause I taught her."

I paid no attention to him and did my best to ignore the memories flashing in my mind of the hot summer day Kick and I had sex on the kitchen floor of his house after he showed me how to change the washer on the tap in that kitchen. "What's with the Tupperware, Mum?" She must have had every single piece she owned on the kitchen bench.

She stopped washing up, turned her body to face me and gave me her full attention, a look of humour crossing her face. "I had a bloody spider in the kitchen and the Tupperware cupboard was open. This was before Kick arrived. Anyway, the damn spider crawled in that cupboard and you know how much

37

I hate spiders... I started madly pulling Tupperware out and onto the floor until I could see the spider. When I saw it, I shut the cupboard to trap it. I was gonna call you to come get it out, but Kick showed up and found it for me."

I spun around to face him. "Did you kill it?"

His face softened and he murmured, "No, Evie, I didn't kill it. I remember."

"I wanted him to, but he reminded me how much you hate that so he took it outside for me. Goodness gracious, I have no idea why you won't just let us kill them," my mother said.

Undeniable warmth spread through me that he'd done that.

For me.

And that he'd remembered.

I was still facing Kick and he whispered, "I get it, baby."

My breathing picked up at his words. More memories flashed in my mind - Kick and I at about sixteen, telling each other our deepest fears and heartaches. He was the only one who got it, who knew why I was so against killing spiders.

Shelly loved spiders.

I stared up at him, lost in the memories, and then I took a deep breath and turned back to face mum. Brushing off what she'd said, I changed the subject. "I can't stay long, but do you need me to do anything or pick anything up at the store for you?"

"No, I stopped at the supermarket on my way home from work yesterday and picked up some groceries."

I smiled at her. "That's good, Mum."

She returned my smile. "I'm trying, Evie, I promise."

I reached out and squeezed her hand. "I know."

Her face turned sombre. "How are you doing? After the funeral?"

"I can't believe he's gone." My voice choked up as Jeremy's

38

face flashed through my mind. For a moment there I'd had a reprieve from the memories.

I watched as she swallowed hard and realised this would be stirring her memories and regrets up, too. She nodded quickly and then turned back to the sink and busied herself with dishes again. Mum wasn't the kind of woman who ever liked to talk about her daughter's death, in fact I could hardly recall having any real conversations of substance about it with her. I waited to see if she would say anything further but she didn't, and I let her have that. It was probably not the best choice but I'd never pushed her to talk.

Turning, I looked up at Kick. "Thanks for helping Mum."

He nodded, his intense gaze never leaving mine. "Anytime."

When he didn't move to let me out of the kitchen, I widened my eyes and nodded at the entry in a let-me-out-of-here gesture. He took his time but he finally stepped aside, and I brushed past him. Without a backwards glance I left the house and hurried to my car. My mind and body were tangled with desire and confusion, and the sooner I got out of Kick's space, the better.

As I opened my car door, a hand grasped my arm and stopped me. I turned in surprise to find Kick behind me.

Shit.

"What?" I demanded.

"Your mum's doing well."

"You came after me to tell me *that*?"

With a shake of his head, he said, "No."

We stood watching each other, not saying a word. I truly didn't know what he wanted after all this time. "Yeah, she's doing okay at the moment. I got her to see someone and start working through all her shit. Finally. Only took nineteen years, but she's getting to the point where she's leaving the house more and more."

"That's good. I hated watching her shut herself away like that."

"Yeah," I said softly, and then asked, "What do you want, Kick?"

"You."

Unmistakable heat flowed between us at his statement and I sucked in a breath. We'd been here before and Kick did not want me. He only thought he did. "No, you don't. You want what you think we can be, but as soon as you can have that, you'll pull away, so why bother starting something we both know will only end badly?"

"That's the past, Evie. I've changed and realised I want you in my life. Give me a chance, baby."

Everything in me screamed to say yes, but my head knew better. "No."

I didn't wait for him to say anything further before getting in the car and shutting the door. I turned the key in the ignition and attempted to ignore him, but he tapped on the window until I finally put it down.

He leant his head in the car and said, "I was wrong, Evie."

"When?"

"Three years ago when I told you I didn't want you in my world." His eyes held the truth in his statement; I saw regret, but I couldn't let that sway me. Just because he regretted his choice didn't mean he'd end up making a different one this time if I let him back in.

"Well, it's too late now," I dismissed him.

He shook his head. "Life's too short to say shit like that. And it's too fuckin' short not to go after what you want. And I'm telling you now, baby, I want you, and I'm gonna get what I want." And there was Kick's trademark stubbornness. I could

40

tell from the way his eyes bore into mine that he was trying to force me to go along with what *he* wanted.

I stared at him, unsure of what to say to that. And when he moved his hand to cradle my face and rub my lips with his thumb, I sat there and let him do it. He'd taken me completely by surprise.

He let me go and straightened. Tapping the top of my car, he said, "I'll see you soon." And then I watched him walk back into my mother's house, my eyes hardly able to shift from his ass.

Fuck.

Chapter Four

Kick

I sat at the bar of the clubhouse and stared at Nitro as he told me about the bike engine he was rebuilding. His words drifted in and out as my concentration bounced between him and thoughts of Evie. It had been a week since I'd seen her at her Mum's. I'd purposely left her alone, because if there was one thing I knew about her, it was how much she hated being pushed into doing something. After all these years, I knew when to push and when to back off.

"Kick, are you fucking listening to me?" Nitro broke through my thoughts.

I took a swig of my beer before answering him. "Sorry, brother."

He finished his beer and motioned to Brittany to bring him another. "All good, man, I know you've been through some shit the last week. But you should drop by my house one day and take a look at the engine. Could do with some help, 'cause I've heard you know your shit around engines."

Nitro and I weren't close but I'd recently realised how much we had in common and maybe helping him with his engine would stop me fucking thinking about Jeremy and Evie so much. "Yeah, I will."

Brittany brought Nitro his drink and leant across the bar, flashing her huge tits at him. I didn't have much respect for her but she was the best bar bitch we had. "You think you could convince King to let me redecorate the bar?" she asked us, eager eyes flicking between the two of us.

Nitro grinned at her. He often used her when he wanted a quick lay and I knew they had an easy friendship. "Darlin', I could try and convince King of anything if you let me fuck you the way I want," he said with a wink. He reached across the bar and traced her cleavage with his finger, which caused her to close her eyes and moan.

"Fuck, you two, get a fuckin' room," I snapped, and gulped the rest of my beer down.

Nitro slipped his hand into her top. Eyeing me he said, "I would if she'd play the way I want to, but she never does."

She slapped his hand away. "I told you I'm not interested in that, Nitro. You'll have to find some other slut to let you do that."

He shrugged. "You'll have to find someone else to convince King then, babe, 'cause no play means no help from me. Besides, I don't think any of us could give a fuck about paint and furniture and shit like that."

Brittany cast an unconvinced gaze around the room. "So you don't care about the ugly cream paint that is peeling in some parts, or the out-dated wood tables and chairs, or the fact the couches in here obviously have seen better days and too much cum? I hate sitting on those couches because I know that nearly all of you boys have each fucked more than a handful of bitches on them and spread your germs everywhere. And what about the plants that are dying in here because whoever picked them chose the wrong plants for inside and no one ever waters them besides me? Oh, and your Storm logo on the wall behind the bar needs to be redone because it's all worn and shit."

I raised my brows at her. "I see you've put a lot of thought into this, but, personally, I couldn't give a shit and I doubt King does, either."

"Give a shit about what?" King's voice sounded behind me.

I jerked my chin at Brittany. "She wants to redecorate. Says it's old and ugly in here. And she hates the cum on the couches."

King laughed. "You want new couches, sweetheart? You and I could christen them."

She rolled her eyes. "Okay, I get it. You don't care what your clubhouse looks like."

King stopped laughing and narrowed his eyes on her. "Tell you what. You figure out a cost for me and I'll think about it, but I want something from you in return."

Fear flickered in her eyes, and she didn't respond. No one ever wanted to owe King anything, especially not a female. I'd heard the stories about what he demanded from women and I didn't blame her for her hesitation.

"Well?" he barked, waiting for her answer.

"I think it'll cost too much," she said, her voice holding no trace of her previous confidence.

He gave her a long, hard look before finally nodding. "Yeah, I thought it might," he said darkly.

I watched her walk away from us, and head towards the other end of the bar. It was fairly clear she couldn't get there fast enough.

Nitro stood. "Gotta hit the head. I'll catch you later."

After he'd left, King asked, "You heard anything around the traps about Silver Hell?"

Had I heard whether they knew it was Storm who'd killed two of their guys?

"Haven't heard a thing."

"Yeah, me either. We need to try and find out more. You able to do that?"

44

I nodded. "I've got some contacts. I'll follow it up for you."

He slapped me on the back. "Good." His gaze shifted from me to track Brittany's moves and he leant on the bar in what seemed like an effort to get a better view. Once he'd had his fill, he looked back at me. "I've got a job for you today. Need you to collect some of our hard-earned cash."

"Who from?"

His gaze had shifted back to Brittany for a moment, but his eyes came straight back to me. "Our coke-loving friend who never fucking wants to pay up. Sort him the fuck out, Kick, 'cause I'm sick of his fucking shit. In fact, if I never have to deal with him again, I would be a very happy man."

King speak —Take him out or ensure he never comes knocking on our door again.

I stood and watched as he continued to track Brittany's moves. That bitch had zero chance of avoiding him now. She'd well and truly caught his attention today. "Consider it done," I said.

He glanced at me. "Good." That was King's signature word to convey his pleasure at his directions being carried out. You never got much more than that from him.

I left him to it, figuring Brittany now had less than fifteen minutes before her shift at the bar ended.

I also figured we'd be getting new paint in here soon.

***

I cut the engine of my bike and assessed the street. I'd never come to Bruno's house to collect before. Usually, I visited the bar he frequented, but I'd gone there earlier and hadn't found him so figured I'd give his home a shot. Bruno lived on a quiet street which was a good thing for me, and even more so today

45

because there was no one around. Not that I really gave a fuck but it did make things easier when there were less witnesses to take care of.

I left my bike and headed to the back door. I'd almost expected him to have a dog to harass me but he didn't. His yard was a fucking mess of overgrown grass and rubbish that had just been dumped out the back. Filthy, junkie pig.

The back door was unlocked which I'd been counting on. The number of idiots who left their back doors unlocked never failed to amaze me. I entered and the smell of pot hit me instantly. I fucking hoped he wasn't entertaining; I really didn't want to have to deal with more than him today.

I'd entered through the laundry room, which then took me to a hallway and I followed that along until I came to the living room. Bruno sat on the couch staring at the television, sucking hard on his joint like he couldn't get what he needed from it. He was so engrossed in the joint and the television he didn't hear me approach.

I walked behind the couch and smacked him on the back of his head. He jumped a fucking mile and almost propelled himself into the television before turning around to glare at me.

"What the fuck, Kick?" he demanded, still clinging to that fucking joint as if it were worth a lot to him. I guessed it probably was. This dickhead had nothing in his life but drugs, debt and a whole lot of regret.

I advanced on him and he must have read the look on my face clearly because worry crossed his and he began backing up to get away from me. "You think you can escape this?" I asked as I kept walking towards him.

"Escape what?" he said on a beg. If there was one thing Bruno was good at, it was convincing himself his problems weren't as bad as they were.

46

I moved into his personal space, glaring down at him. "Escape the world of hurt you're about to be in."

Terror filled his eyes. "No! I've got the money!"

"Really? You expect me to believe that, Bruno? You never have the fuckin' money."

His head bobbed up and down rapidly as he nodded at me. "I have it! It's in my house...I'll go and get it for you."

He attempted to move, and I raised my hand to grip his shoulder and halt him. "Not so fast, motherfucker. You don't move unless I say you can move. We got that?"

He gulped and sweat beaded on his forehead. As he moved his arm to wipe the sweat away, he agreed, "Yes."

I let go of his shoulder and asked, "Where is this money? What room?"

"My bedroom."

I pulled my gun out and aimed it at his forehead. His eyes widened and I took in the accelerated rise and fall of his chest. "You lead the way, but the minute you don't do as I say, I'll shoot. And it won't be to kill to start with. We clear?"

He tripped over his words to get them out fast. "Yes, I get it, Kick, but there's no need to - "

I pressed my gun hard against his forehead. "There's always a need, Bruno. With dickheads like you, anyway. Now shut the fuck up and start fuckin' walking."

He did as I said, and I followed closely behind as he led me to his bedroom. The house was a fucking mess with crap strewn all over the floors. His bedroom was no different. As he began rummaging through his drawers, the only sounds that could be heard in the house were the ticking of his bedside clock and his breaths that were coming hard and fast now.

I moved to stand behind him and pressed the gun into his back. "I hope to fuck you're not looking for a gun," I said, not

47

really expecting him to be that smart, but you just never fucking knew.

He shook his head. "No, the money is in here somewhere. I've just got to find which socks I hid it in."

"You hid your money in your fuckin' socks?"

He turned his head to glare at me. "Well, where the hell else would I hide it, smartass?"

"What the fuck did you just say to me?" I bellowed. Assholes like him annoyed the absolute fuck out of me. First, he was too stupid to keep his shit straight, then he had the balls to think he could get out of dealing with the consequences, and to top it off, he wanted to call me fucking names? Fuck that shit.

The look of recognition that crossed his face was priceless. That moment when your target realises just how much shit they're actually in never failed to pump excitement through my veins. "Shit, sorry, dude. I didn't mean it."

I raised my gun and shot at the roof. What I really wanted to do was shoot him, but I needed to get that money first so the roof was the next best thing to hurry him along. Pointing the gun back at him, I roared, "Hurry the fuck up. I don't have all day."

Sweat had started to take over his face and his shirt stuck to the sweat on his body. He began rummaging faster until, eventually, he located the cash. Dragging it out of his sock faster than a virgin ejaculated, he shoved it at me. "Take it!"

"Calm the fuck down," I suggested as I took the wads of twenties and tens from him. "And let's move this to your kitchen table so I can count it." He owed us six grand and I wanted to make sure it was all here before I took care of him.

Once he'd given it all to me, he began walking to the kitchen. I indicated for him to sit at the table and then I sat opposite him and started counting. He surprised the hell out of me by managing to keep his mouth shut while I did this. Bruno usually babbled shit the whole time when I came to collect cash.

I counted slowly. The bastard had come out in me today and I enjoyed feeling his fear while he waited for me to finish.

He was fifty bucks short.

I glared at him before pointing my gun at his foot and shooting.

He screamed out in pain as blood started going everywhere. Wild eyes landed on mine and he yelled out, "Why the fuck did you do that?"

"You're short," I said calmly, leaning back into my chair and extending my leg out to stretch it.

"Well, you should have just said so. I've got more!" His face had contorted in pain and he gripped his leg tightly. Sweat now poured down his face and his clothes were a wet, sweaty mess.

"I shouldn't have to fuckin' say so, Bruno. You should know by now that when I come to collect my money I want all of it. What I don't want is to be fucked around."

"It's hardly fucking you around, asshole," he muttered. "How was I to know that sock was fifty bucks short?"

I shot his other foot and watched him writhe in pain. "Where the fuck is the rest of your money stashed? And don't screw me around anymore," I demanded.

He struggled to get the words out. Jerking his chin at the kitchen pantry, he stuttered, "In there, top shelf in the brown container at the back."

Pushing my chair back, I raised my brows and said, "Funny how bullets encourage honesty, isn't it?"

"Fuck you," he spat out, clearly not giving a shit if he pissed me off anymore.

I ignored him and reached up into the cupboard in search of the brown container. My eyes widened in surprise when I

49

opened it. I whistled and murmured, "Fuck me, Bruno. You've been holding out on me."

There had to be twenty grand in here.

"Just take fifty and leave me the fuck alone."

My gaze flicked to him. Was he deluded? "You really think I'm gonna walk out of here today without this cash?"

His fight wasn't gone. "I swear to fucking God, Kick, if you take my money I will hunt you down for it."

I chuckled and cocked my head to the side, giving him a questioning look. "You really think you'll be alive to hunt me down?"

Finally, he realised the depth of shit he was in today. He pushed his chair back and attempted to stand. I watched as he collapsed onto the floor, his body twisting in pain as he did so.

I walked to him and looked down over him. "You've been screwing our club around for years now, motherfucker, and my president is finally done with you. And besides, you're a junkie criminal who preys on the fuckin' elderly and disabled so I'd be ridding the world of a scumbag we can do without."

Hi voice pleaded with me. "Take the money, Kick. You'll never hear from me again. And I promise not to rob or hurt those people anymore." His meaningless words fell out of his mouth. I knew they meant nothing, because Bruno was a creature of habit and he'd never made good on any of his promises before.

"It's too late for more shitty promises." I looked around his kitchen. "I won't miss chasing you for cash. Between the dive of a bar you drink your life away in and this dump, you've really outdone yourself in life."

He spat at my feet before giving me a filthy look. "Fuck you!"

I pointed my gun at his forehead and pulled the trigger.

50

He fell backwards as blood went everywhere.

I pointed the gun at his chest and fired three more bullets into him. Just to be certain King got his wish to never have to deal with him again.

Then I grabbed the money from the brown container, and the money off the table, stashed it in my jacket and left the way I'd come in.

Bruno's body may not be discovered for days, weeks even, depending on the stench it caused. He had no family or real friends I was aware of, and in the world we lived in, no one gave much of a shit about anyone unless you were part of a club or gang. Bruno belonged to no one and so no one would care.

That was the cold hard truth of our world.

***

Two hours later, after I'd been home and sorted Bruno's cash out and then delivered King's amount to him, I pulled up at the cemetery. I had no idea why, but I'd felt the pull there. It wasn't where Jeremy was, his family had organised for him to be cremated. As I left my bike and began walking across the grass, it hit me.

Shelly's here.

I'd almost made it to her grave when a little old lady stumbled and fell on the path in front of me. She landed on her knees and struggled to get back up again. I quickly walked to her so I could kneel down and help her up.

"Are you okay?" I asked, assessing her to see if she'd done much damage.

Her eyes came to mine and while I saw a small amount of pain there, she smiled. "I'm a silly old fool," she said softly, "I'm always falling over these days but I haven't hurt myself. If you could just help me up, I'll keep going."

She raised her arms and I placed my hands under her shoulders and helped her up. A little unsteady on her feet to start with, she regained her balance, but I kept hold of her until I could verify she wouldn't fall again.

"Can you stand on your own now?" I asked, watching her intently to make sure she could.

Nodding, she said, "Yes, I'll be fine. Thank you for your help. It's hard to find good people like you these days."

I ignored her incorrect assumption about me being good and slowly let her go. When I could see she was all right on her own, I asked, "Where's your car?"

She gave me a smile. "I can manage on my own."

I shook my head and reached for her elbow to help guide her. "No, I want to make sure you get there without falling again."

"Thank you. Even my own son doesn't look out for me like this," she murmured as we began walking.

The journey to her car took some time because she couldn't walk very fast, but that was okay with me. I was just glad when we got there and she hadn't fallen. Once I had her settled in the car, I shut her door and stepped back. She smiled and gave me a wave as she drove off. I stood lost in my thoughts while I watched her go, and didn't hear the approaching footsteps on the gravel.

"Kick?"

I spun around.

Evie.

"What are you doing here?" she asked before I said anything.

"I really don't know." In that moment, I felt lost. Suddenly, and out of nowhere, I felt alone in this world, like I had no one in my corner.

Fuck, what the hell is wrong with me?

She frowned. "Are you okay?"

I scrubbed my face and blinked my eyes a couple of times. "Yeah, I don't know what the fuck it is, but I'm okay."

The hardness she tended to look at me with these days eased a little and she said, "It's Jeremy's death, I'd say. I feel the same way."

I didn't say anything, just stood and watched her. Fuck, I could watch her forever and never grow tired. She seemed so vulnerable at the moment, though, and I wanted to wrap her in my arms, but I knew that would be a bad move so I kept my arms by my side and stayed silent.

Her body relaxed and she raked her fingers through her long hair. "Why did you two have that falling out years ago?"

She caught me off guard. I hadn't been expecting that. My body stiffened and I blew out a long breath. "It's a long story, Evie, and there's no point rehashing it. What's done is done, and Jeremy's gone so I can't fuckin' fix it now."

"I feel like whatever happened between you two had something to do with me, and I hate that. I hate thinking that I came between you guys."

Fuck.

I hated the tinge of sadness I could hear in her voice, and the way her body slumped.

"It wasn't your fault. We were just stubborn assholes and couldn't see past a disagreement. It was a fuckin' waste of a good friendship and if I could go back and change it, I would. Instead, I have to live with it now. Live with the fact I fucked up."

She shifted on her feet and slung her handbag over her shoulder. "Okay, I can respect that, and I'm glad it wasn't because of me." She took a step away from me and added, "I'll catch you, Kick. I'm gonna go visit Shelly now."

I'll catch you, Kick.

Those fucking words warmed my heart.

"See you, baby."

She blessed me with one last smile and then headed towards Shelly's grave.

Fuck, that shit with Jeremy would haunt me for the rest of my life.

***

Kick
30 years old — 5 years ago

"What the fuck are you doing, asshole?" Jeremy's thunderous voice echoed around the room. He'd just barged into my house and we stood glaring at each other in my living room. I knew why he was here.

Evie.

She and I had just gotten back together, so of course he was in my face.

He loved her as much as I did.

I glared at him. "I'm fucking the woman I love, and, one day, I'm gonna make her my wife. I walked away from her once and I'm not gonna let anything or anyone come between us again. I'm not gonna let you come between us again."

His fist connected with my jaw a moment later, and I stumbled back, caught by surprise. Jeremy and I had never had a physical fight before. I held my jaw as he roared, "How the fuck can you talk about Evie like that?"

"Like what?"

"I asked you what you're doing, and you say you're fucking her? What kind of a pig are you, anyway, Kick? Most men would say they're dating her, not fucking her."

I spat out some blood and reminded him I wasn't like most men.
"I'm an asshole, remember? That's how assholes obviously speak."

"You were never an asshole before, Kick. Storm has made you that
way and I fail to grasp what Evie sees in you."

"Well, it's a good thing you're not Evie, then. Don't try and come
between us, Jeremy. I swear to fuckin' God, if you do . . . if you fuck
this up for us, it won't be pretty between you and me."

He fumed. His body tensed as if he was about to punch me again
and the vein in his neck pulsed. "Things haven't been pretty between us
for a while now and this is the end of it for me, unless you walk away
from her."

What the fuck?

"You're fuckin' kidding me! You'd throw our friendship away over
this?"

"No, Kick, you pretty much threw our friendship away when you
joined Storm. When you sold your soul to the devil and said to hell with
everything and everyone. If you drag Evie into that world, I will spend
the rest of my days fighting to get her out of it."

I moved closer to him. Into his face. "I suggest you get the hell out
of my house and never come back. I **never** *want to see your face again,"*
I snarled, my eyes boring into his, screaming at him how much I meant
every fucking word I'd said.

I was done with him.

He stood rooted to the spot for a moment, his eyes searching mine. I
saw it. I saw the moment where he decided he was done, too. Something
flashed in his eyes and he took a step away from me. "Done," he
snapped. And then he added, "If you love her like you say you do, you
won't drag her down with you. You won't give her a life of shit and
grime. Think about that."

And then he was gone.

And I'd been thinking about that for five fucking years.

I'd let those thoughts convince me to walk away three years ago, but the pull to her was too strong to resist any longer.

As much as I now believed every word Jeremy had spoken to be true, I *was* a selfish bastard and wanted Evie with me.

I couldn't deny it even if I tried.

Chapter Five

Evie

Despair swirled around me, and the four walls of the room closed in on me as my father admitted his latest fuck up to me. As I stood in his sorry excuse for a home, I squeezed my eyes shut and wished we could go back nineteen years and change the course of history. Change the fact he lived alone with threadbare carpets, worn couches with holes in them, clothes that hung off him because he didn't care about eating, a career he'd let go of, and a fucking gambling addiction that ruined any chance of changing and improving his life.

"Fuck, Dad . . . how did this happen? You were doing so much better." My eyes pleaded with him. I needed something, anything to give me hope this could be fixed. My gut knew, though. Knew this was what always happened, this was just the never-ending cycle of addiction that, once it had you in its grips, would never let you go. Not if you really didn't want it to.

He hung his head.

Shame bathed his face.

Defeat clothed his body.

The man who'd raised me had vanished and in his place stood this father who I struggled to understand and love. I would always love him deep down, but it was more a reflex emotion. These days, love didn't come easily...I had to work to love him.

He looked back up at me, his face more ravaged than I'd ever seen. When he finally spoke, he almost gutted me. "Baby,

I need help."

My father had never asked for help.

Never.

Not when my sister had died, not when my mother had cheated on him, not when he'd lost his job and had to take shitty casual jobs to pay his bills, and never for his gambling addiction.

His words pierced my heart and tears pricked my eyes.

Love knocked on my soul and I knew in that moment, I would do anything to help my father.

"How much do you owe?"

His eyes shut and he drew a long breath. Opening them again, he said, "Ten grand."

My heart dropped into my stomach.

Ten grand.

Where the hell were we gonna come up with that kind of money?

My legs nearly buckled under me so I sat on the couch behind me, rested my elbows on my knees and dropped my head into my hands. This shit was fucked and although my brain scrambled to find a way out for him, it was coming up empty.

Silence filled the room until, eventually, I lifted my head to ask him, "How long have you got to pay it?"

"One week," he whispered just loud enough for me to hear.

Holy shit.

My heart almost beat out of my chest and fear sliced through me. There was no way we could come up with that kind of money in a week. But I wasn't the type of woman to stare defeat in the face and throw in the towel without a fight.

I got my shit together and stood. "Leave it with me, Dad. I'll talk to some people."

Hope flitted across his face. "Yeah?"

"Yeah. But this only happens if you're going to admit you

have a problem and get some help for it." I stared hard at him, waiting.

He hesitated for a moment and I stilled. Surely he wouldn't deny his problem any longer? But then again, my father was a stubborn and proud man, and he'd lived in denial for a long time now.

Relief filled me when he finally spoke. "Yes, I have a problem. I don't know how or where to get help but I will find it." The brokenness in his voice told me everything I needed to know. He'd hit rock bottom. And as much as that pained me, it was possibly the best thing for him because now, finally, he would search for a way out.

"Dad, I'm a counsellor. Remember? I'll find you someone who will help you."

His eyebrows drew together in a frown. "I thought you only counselled kids."

"I do, but I know other counsellors."

Nodding, he murmured, "Okay, Evie, you find me someone and I'll work with them." He paused for a moment before adding, "I know I've let you down over the years and that I've never admitted my addiction... but I need things to change. I want my life back." His voice cracked and he stole another piece of my heart. We'd all lost so much back then but my father had lost the most.

"I know, Dad. We all want you to have your life back," I said softly.

His eyes reached deep inside me and he whispered, "Thank you."

***

I left Dad's house and drove around in circles for a while,

59

thinking. Wondering where the hell I would find ten grand. Eventually, I found myself on my sister's doorstep. She answered the door, looking a little bewildered.

"Evie! Come in," she said, ushering me into her home.

"What's wrong?" I asked, because she really did seem frazzled.

"I'll tell you over a drink," she replied and waved her hand, indicating I should enter.

Julie was two years older than me and lived alone. I hadn't been to her house in years but it didn't appear to have changed much. She still had the cream walls she seemed to love, the country style wood furniture I couldn't stand, but that she adored, and plants scattered everywhere. Her home had that lived-in feel, though, and I loved that.

She took me into her kitchen and offered me coffee. "Have you just finished work now?" she asked, glancing at the clock that read seven thirty.

I shook my head. "No, I finished hours ago but I went to see Dad and have been driving around ever since."

Her eyes widened. "Shit, that doesn't sound good. We definitely need coffee for this . . . or perhaps something stronger?"

"Coffee is good, thanks."

She got her Nespresso going and said, "Spill. Tell me what he's done now."

I sighed and sat on one of her bar stools, slumping onto the counter. "He has gotten himself into debt again and has one week to pay back the money. I told him I would help him find it. The good news is that he's finally realised he needs help."

My words caused her to still and stare at me in shock. "What the hell will happen if you don't?"

My heart rate picked up. I'd been working hard not to think

about that. "I honestly don't know but I'm thinking that the kind of person who has ten grand to lend someone to bet with can't be good news. Especially not if you end up owing him with no way of paying it back."

"Oh my God," she muttered as she made the coffee and brought it over to me. Settling herself on a stool, she asked, "Have you got anyone in mind to ask?"

"You're my first port of call. I figured I'd start with family and work out from there." I looked at her hopefully but her face told me everything I needed to know. She didn't have it.

"I'm so sorry, but I'm struggling financially at the moment. That's actually the reason I was looking so strange when you knocked on the door. I've got credit card bills piling up and then today I found out I won't have a job in a month."

I reached out my hand to hold hers. Squeezing it, I said, "I'm so sorry. If I can help you at all, I will."

She sighed. "God, I am such a bitch."

I frowned. "Why?"

"Because you are such a good human being, and I have treated you like shit since Shelly died."

Shit, tears threatened to fall at her words. She was right — she *had* been a bitch, but I figured we'd all coped with Shelly's death in our own way, and hers was to shut her family out.

When I didn't respond, she continued, "And now, a week after I make contact after years of shutting you out, you offer to help me in my hour of need."

My eyes glistened and I smiled at her. "It's what family is for. Ours might be messed up and all, but maybe we can find a way to put it back together."

"I think it'll take some time, Evie," she warned.

Nodding, I agreed. "Yeah, I know, but if there's one thing Jeremy's death has taught me, it's that we don't have all the

61

time in the world."

"And how does forgiveness factor into all that? 'Cause unless we can all forgive each other, I don't see anything changing."

"Forgiveness isn't for the other person, Julie, it's for us. It lets *us* move forward, out of our hate and anger at the other person. And I don't think it necessarily means you forget. You just choose to move past that bad stuff so you can have more good stuff in your life."

She raised a brow at me. "Sounds like you're speaking from experience, little sister?"

"I guess I am. I wouldn't say I hated Kick after he walked away, but I was so mad at him for giving up on us and it took me a long time to work through those feelings. I realised *he* didn't know how bad I was feeling, so the only person it was affecting and hurting was *me*. That's when I decided to forgive him, just so I could let those feelings go."

"And now?"

"What do you mean?"

"Well, now that you've forgiven him, would you take him back if he asked?"

"Like I said, just because I've forgiven doesn't mean I've forgotten. I didn't go through all that to not learn a lesson there. Unless Kick has changed dramatically in some things, I won't take him back."

"The way you're speaking makes me think he's trying to get you back. Is he?"

I took a deep breath. "Yeah, he is."

"I said it to you the other day, I truly think you two were made for each other, Evie. At least give him one more go."

"I don't know if my heart can take another round," I whispered, my heart already hurting at the thought of *not* giving him another go, but at the same time guarding itself from more hurt.

She drank some of her coffee, and nodded. "I get it. Love's a scary thing when you've been stung before. But you've given me another go."

I smiled. "You're different. You're family."

She leant closer to me. "So is Kick, Evie. Haven't you worked that out by now?"

Shit, she had a point.

When I left her home an hour later, my thoughts were completely consumed by Kick. How long would it take for him to wear me down? I'd do my best to stick to my guns but I knew if he kept pushing, I'd eventually cave. He'd left soul prints on me. I could never say no to Kick . . . I could never deny the pull his heart had to mine.

***

The next day I dropped by my mum's house after work to check on her again. I was surprised to see Kick's brother's work ute out the front. Braden was a builder and I doubted my mother needed a one.

"Mum," I yelled out as I entered her house, "why is Braden here?"

"Evie, we're in the living room. Come and join us," she yelled back, so I headed in that direction.

A minute later, I came face to face with Kick.

Not Braden.

Kick.

Shit.

"Where's Braden?" I blurted out.

"What?" Mum asked, clearly confused.

I jerked my thumb in the direction of the driveway.

"Braden's ute is out front. I was wondering where he is."

Kick had been sitting on the couch opposite Mum, but he stood and came towards me. I tried so hard not to let my gaze drop to his body, but it was impossible, and a second later I found myself checking out his fitted tee and the muscles straining under it.

Shit.

Eyes up, Evie. Stop looking.

It was useless.

My eyes kept wandering down his body, soaking in the sexiness that was Kick Hanson.

He chuckled and dipped his head so our faces were centimetres apart. "It's all yours, baby, you just say the word," he said, his deep voice causing an explosion of need in me.

Shit.

I placed my hand on his chest and tried to push him away, but, just like the last time, his body didn't budge. He did move his face away, though, but grinned at me as he did it.

He knows I am close.

So damn close.

I ignored what he'd said. "What are you here for today, Kick?"

He shrugged. "Do I need a reason? I remember when I used to practically live at this house."

"That was a long time ago."

"Yeah, well, maybe I miss those days."

Regret flared deep within me. "I do, too, Kick, but we can't go back. That's not how life works."

His eyes revealed his own regret, and we stood silently watching each other for a couple of moments. Finally, he said, "Yeah." Taking a step away from me, he turned back to face Mum and said, "Thanks for the drink, Loretta. I'll see you soon."

"Thanks for dropping in," Mum replied, "come back whenever you want."

He nodded and then faced me again. Stepping closer, he reached out to cup my cheek and ran his thumb over my lip. "We can't go back, Evie, but we can sure as fuck go forward."

Kick had always been able to turn me on with just a look or his voice or the lightest of touches, and now was no different. His touch, his voice, and his words melded together and caused desire to spread to every nerve ending in my body.

The other thing he'd always been able to do was read me well. Awareness flickered in his eyes and the corners of his mouth twitched in the slightest of smiles. He traced my lips one more time and then he let me go and said, "I'll see you soon, too, baby."

I wrapped my arms around my body as I watched him go.

Hell, Kick Hanson had me.

"Evie," Mum cut into my thoughts, and I spun around to look at her. "What's up?"

"Huh?" God, my brain had turned to mush after Kick got to it.

"Well, you came over, so I figure you wanted something."

I went and sat on the couch with her. "No, I just came to see how you were," I said, glancing at her to see how she was doing. Usually, tiredness marred her face, but lately she'd been doing better. After Shelly's death, Mum had sunk into a deep depression and never really recovered. She'd retreated within and hardly left the house. It was only recently she'd started to really come out of it and seemed much happier these days. But it took a lot of work on her behalf, and I knew that, so I did my best to help her out whenever I could and checked in on her regularly.

"Thank you," she said, giving me a sad smile, "How are you, baby? I worry about you."

Her words caused a flush of happiness through my body. One of the side effects of her depression was an inability to care for her kids the way a mother should. She'd been unable to show us much affection and that had lasted for years. These days she gave us random pieces of affection so when she did, I grabbed it with both hands and held tight.

"I'll be okay. You know what it's like. I've just gotta take it one day at a time."

We sat in silence for a little while and then she astounded me by opening up in a way she never had. "One day at a time is all you have to do. But don't do what I did, Evie. If you're struggling, go and see someone to help you. I closed down on you all, and that was the absolute worst thing I could have done. Most of the time, you will probably just want to be left alone, and while you do need that, you also need to talk about what you're going through. Not all the time, but don't shut down. Promise me you won't do that."

"I promise," I whispered, my voice catching in my throat at her rare openness.

Maybe after all these years, I'd finally get my mum back.

***

I shut my eyes and let myself slide deeper into the bath water. Darkness surrounded me except for the flickering of some candles I'd set around the bathroom. Lavender for relaxation.

It'd been a long day, and after leaving Mum's house this afternoon I'd come home, hoping to sink into the couch and not leave it all night. Best-laid plans never worked out, though. My

66

neighbour had called me in a panic. Her washing machine had flooded her laundry and she needed help with her kids while she dealt with her emergency. Three hours later, I'd traipsed home even more exhausted.

Thoughts of my father and his predicament filled my mind as I lay in the bath. As much as I tried to force them out, at least just for the duration of my bath, I couldn't stop them coming. I'd contacted my bank today and begged for a loan, but seeing as I already had a maxed out credit card and a personal loan on my car, they wouldn't lend me anymore. The two thousand dollars I had saved would hardly help my father so I'd then asked some friends if they could lend me any money but the most they could come up with was another thousand. I had six more days to figure this out and not many people left to ask.

Shit.

I sat up in the bath, water sloshing everywhere because I moved so quickly. Nausea hit my gut and I had to take some deep breaths to get my breathing under control.

What the hell am I going to do?

What the hell is my father going to do?

As I sat there, with my hands gripping the sides of the bath and my concentration focused on regaining my breaths, a loud knock on the front door filled the silence in my house.

Who the hell would be knocking on my door at ten o'clock at night?

I stayed in the bath, waiting to see if they went away, but when they knocked again, I pushed myself up and stepped out of the bath. Wrapping my towel around me without even drying myself off, I stalked to the front of the house.

When I got to the front door, I abruptly stopped.

Was I seriously going to answer the door at this time of night wrapped in a freaking towel?

Before I could even process that question and answer it, the person on the other side called out. "Evie, it's Kick. Open up."

Oh my god, he had to be kidding me.

Without any further thought, I yanked the door open and glared at him.

His gaze travelled down my body and then back up to meet my eyes. Stepping forward, he raised one arm up and leant it against the doorjamb. "Sweetheart, you're a sight for sore fuckin' eyes," he said.

I huffed out a breath and shook my head at him. "What are you doing here at this time of night, Kick?"

"What? No hello? No invitation in?" His tone was playful, flirtatious, and I knew we were heading into dangerous territory.

I jerked my chin at the door. "Shut it after you," I said and then began walking down my hall. "I'll meet you in the kitchen in a minute," I yelled out as I made my way into my bedroom to put some clothes on.

His boots sounded behind me. "Don't need to get changed on my account," he said, his sexy voice causing me to shiver as it drifted across my skin.

I ignored him and continued to the bedroom. No way would Kick and I be having a conversation with me wrapped only in a towel.

When I met him in the kitchen a couple of minutes later, he was sitting at the table with his legs stretched out in front of him and his arms crossed over his chest.

I arched a brow as I sat with him. "You look comfortable there."

"You do that to me," he murmured pensively. He appeared to have something on his mind tonight.

"Do what to you?"

68

He sat forward and rested his elbows on his knees and cradled his chin in one hand. "Being around you calms me, baby." His eyes held mine, and time stood still for a moment.

Memories rushed me.

Kick filled so many memories of mine, and his voice and presence triggered an avalanche I couldn't stop. My body shivered as they hit me, as the emotions engulfed me.

I took a deep breath. "It doesn't calm *me*," I said softly.

He frowned. "In a good way or a bad way?" He seemed genuinely interested in my answer.

"I'm not sure," I said softly and then asked, "What did you want to talk to me about?"

He raised his brow. "You're not even gonna offer me a drink?"

"No drink. Just spill so we can talk, and then you can leave."

He shifted to lean forward in his chair. "When are you gonna get that I'm not going anywhere?"

"When are *you* gonna get that *I'm* not interested?"

He smirked and said, "You talk a good game, baby, but you are *more* than fuckin' interested."

"Just start talking, Kick," I said, impatient for him to get his words out.

He paused for a second and his face grew serious. "Can we put all the bullshit aside and be honest with each other for a minute?" His eyes implored me to say yes.

I hesitated. Honesty could lead me to trouble here. But after everything we'd ever been through together, he deserved that, at least. I nodded. "Okay." My voice was anything but sure.

"I want to give us another go," he said, "and I need to know if I've got a shot at making that happen."

My stomach knotted. A mixture of desire and concern.

Before I could reply, he reminded me, "No bullshit, Evie. I know you're still pissed at me, but do you think you can move past that?"

Sometimes in life you tell yourself you don't want something that you really do. And if you tell yourself that for long enough you actually end up believing it. I'd been telling myself for three long years that I didn't want Kick. And I'd grown to believe it. But sitting here with him now, and stripping back the bullshit, I knew deep in my heart I *did* want him.

Only a couple of minutes had passed while we sat in silence, but it felt like more. Finally, I said, "I want you, Kick, I've always wanted you, but I don't know how we would make it work. And you know me, I'm a 'how' person. If I can't get my head around how something is going to work, I can't do it."

"You think too much, baby," he said, still staring at me, willing me to want the same thing he did.

"Well, you don't think enough," I accused, my voice rising.

"I do when it's needed, but this . . ." he thumped his hand against his chest, and his voice grew more forceful when he continued, "this is in here. It doesn't need thought."

"You know what?" I said as I leant forward, moving my face closer to his, "I can feel it as much as I want in *here*," I thumped *my* chest, "but that means shit if we go back to what we were and change nothing."

He didn't say anything, just sat quietly watching me. By the looks of it, he was thinking now. When his phone began ringing a moment later, he answered it with a look of reluctance. I didn't listen to his conversation but rather left him to go and make myself a cup of tea.

When he joined me in the kitchen, I felt his presence behind me before I heard him.

"I've gotta go but I want to continue this conversation.

Yeah?"

I faced him and slowly nodded. "Okay."

"Tomorrow after you finish work?"

I was about to say yes when I remembered I had to keep calling around trying to find money for my dad. "Shit, I can't after work. I've got stuff to do for my dad and then I think Maree is taking me out."

He frowned. "Is your dad okay?"

I let out a long sigh. "No, he's gotten himself in debt again."

"Fuck," he muttered.

"Yeah, that about covers it."

Some of my hair had fallen across my face, and he reached his hand up to tuck it behind my ear. He let his hand slide down and then he curled it gently around my neck, his thumb rubbing over my throat. My breathing picked up as desire flooded me. I wanted this, but I had to go slow and make sure we figured it all out before we rushed into things.

His head dipped and when his lips brushed mine, need unfurled through my entire body, and I couldn't stop myself even if I'd tried. I stepped forward and pressed my body into his. My hand landed on his chest and then slid up so I could tangle my fingers in his hair and at the same time pull his head closer to mine.

I needed him.

Needed him as close as I could get him.

As our tongues danced and our bodies came together, I knew there'd never be another man I wanted as much as Kick. God knew, I'd tried to find one, but kissing him now, I experienced that knowledge deep in my core and in my soul.

He slowly ended our kiss and rested his forehead against mine. "Fuck, baby, we need to sort this out because I fuckin' need to be inside you."

"I know," I whispered, breathless from his kiss.

We stayed like that for another few moments and then he finally pulled away. "Tomorrow. I don't care if it's fuckin' midnight or later, you and I are going to talk," he said with certainty.

After he'd left, I let the excitement and anticipation work its way through me.

I allowed myself to hope that we could find a way to make this work once and for all.

Chapter Six

Kick

Peter Bishop and I had a strange relationship. I felt like my family owed him a lot for what my father had done to him, and I was sure he hated me for everything my father had taken from him. But I was also certain he hated the fact I knew every dark secret he had and that I had bailed him out on more occasions than he cared to admit.

I stood in his living room and watched the broken man in front of me. Fuck, he'd finally hit rock bottom. I'd never known him to admit he had a problem and that's what he'd just done.

"Who do you owe this time?" I asked, hoping like hell it wasn't the same guy he'd owed last time. I had nothing on that asshole so would struggle to dig Peter out if that was the case.

His eyes held fear when he gave me the name. "Jonathon Gambarro."

"Fucking hell!" I yelled, "Why the fuck did you go to him?"

He hung his head for a moment before looking back up at me with regret. "I was running out of options."

I grabbed the back of my neck and muttered, "Jesus, Peter. How long you got to come up with the money?"

"One week."

Fuck.

I dropped my hand and stalked into his kitchen. Reaching into a cupboard, I grabbed a glass and then grabbed the bottle of bourbon I knew he had stashed in another cupboard. It had been a while since I'd been to Peter's house but he was a man of habit, and, sure enough, the bourbon was still there. I poured myself a drink and downed it in one go.

Peter followed me. "I fucked up, Kick."

I turned my head to look at him, a scowl on my face. "You did more than fuck up this time. Gambarro isn't known for his compassion."

"I don't know what to do. Evie told me she would take care of it, but - "

I cut him off, "Evie's not fuckin' going near this shit fight. I won't have her involved in this. Do not fuckin' tell her who you owe or I swear to fuckin' God I will take you out myself." Anger spread through me at the mere thought he'd even think to involve Evie in this. Did he not have a clue who he was dealing with?

He didn't say a word. A good fucking idea because anything he'd say would be the wrong thing at this point. My fists clenched and I slammed my hand down on the counter in frustration. I stared at him for a long moment, trying desperately to contain my rage, and when I couldn't rein it in any longer, I picked up the glass in front of me and threw it at the wall. "This is the last fuckin' time, Peter!" I yelled at him. " If I drag you out of this, and then find out you've done it again… so help you God because *I* sure as fuck won't be."

He nodded but remained silent.

He knew he'd pushed me to the limit.

He knew I was done.

The debt to his family was paid.

***

74

Four hours later, I sunk down into a couch at the clubhouse bar. Hyde sat in the couch opposite me, his eyes questioning what was wrong. I still wore my anger at Peter plain for everyone to see. "What's up with you?" he asked as he drank some of his beer.

I struggled with sharing my dilemma with him but decided I needed to. Any involvement of mine in this could potentially impact the club. I leant forward and rested my elbows on my knees. "My ex's father owes ten grand to Jonathon Gambarro and the only hope he has of settling the debt is if I step in and help him."

Hyde's face clouded over with displeasure. "And what exactly would that involve?"

"I'd have to threaten him with something. I'd need the debt wiped with no payment involved, so that's the only way to make that happen."

"Fuck, Kick. This is dangerous territory. You really want to get mixed up with Gambarro? I can assure you once you're on his radar he'll have you in his sights and won't rest 'til he takes care of you in whatever way he deems fit."

I blew out a long breath. "I fuckin' know that, Hyde, but what choice do I have? If I don't step in, her father is dead."

"And if you do step in, you're a target going forward." He leant forward. "And the club's a fucking target."

"Yeah."

He shook his head and stood. "Stay out of it, Kick. The club doesn't need any more trouble. We're still waiting to see if Silver Hell connects us with what you and King did the other night; this is more shit we don't need."

Fuck.

***

75

"Please, Kick. I'm desperate," my sister begged me over the phone at three o'clock that afternoon. She needed a babysitter for a couple of hours while she attended her university lecture.

"I can do it, Lina, but fuck, where the hell is Dave?" Her asshole ex-husband always let her down and it pissed me off.

"He's drunk again. He just called me, like five fucking minutes ago, to say he couldn't make it now because he accidentally drank too much at the pub after work." Not only did she sound angry; I could hear the exhaustion in her voice. Fuck, that asshole would be answering to me.

"I'll be there soon," I promised. Hanging up, I eyed Nitro who I'd been talking to about bike engines again, and said, "Sorry man, I've gotta go help my sister out."

"Sure, brother. We good for Saturday?" he asked, watching as I stood.

We'd planned to work on his engine. "Yeah, I'll probably get to your place by eleven."

He gave me a chin lift and I headed out.

When I arrived at Lina's house twenty minutes later, she seemed even more frazzled. My brows knit together. "What's wrong?"

"Dave just called again and said he'd be here after all." She gave me a pained look. "Kick, I don't want him anywhere near the kids, not when he's drunk."

I placed my hand on her upper arm. "I'll take care of him, okay? I don't want you worrying about it. You just go and do your shit and leave Dave to me."

Tears pricked her eyes and she collapsed into my arms. "I don't know how much longer I can do this," she sobbed.

Fuck, things were worse than I realised. "What the fuck's going on, Lina?"

She clung to me and sobbed for a good few minutes before

76

pulling away and wiping her eyes. Sniffling, she admitted, "He does this often. And sometimes he turns up and gets aggressive with me if I won't let him in the house."

"Fuck, me!" I yelled, the anger punching through my body, "Why the fuck didn't you tell me sooner?"

"I didn't want this to happen!" she yelled back. "I wanted to try and sort it out without involving you because I knew you'd resort to violence to fix it."

I scowled at her. "Sometimes the only thing that works is violence."

She hung her head for a moment and then gave me her eyes again. Sad eyes. "I know you won't get this, but I still love him. After everything he's done, I still love him, and even though I know we aren't good together and can never go back to what we had, I don't want you to hurt him," she said softly, her words pleading with me to understand.

I roughly rubbed the back of my neck. "Shit, Lina. You're right, I don't get it. The guy fucked around on you, he's a shit father, and you want mercy for him? Even after he's gotten aggressive with you?"

Her lips spread into a thin line. "Some people don't know how to do better, Kick. For some, their best is our worst, and it's not always their fault," she said softly, calmly.

My eyes widened. "Don't sprout that psych bullshit at me that you're learning, 'cause I'm not fuckin' interested in excuses. How can you stand here and cry on my shoulder about him one minute and then turn around and defend him the next?"

She sighed. "If I went through life holding onto the shit people have done to me, I'd be an angry and depressed person. I have to let it go . . . for me, not them. And sometimes you can love and hate someone at the same time. I choose to let both in, to not deny my feelings and only concentrate on the bad. And as far as crying on your shoulder, yeah, I've reached a point where I'm feeling overwhelmed. Sometimes you just need a good cry and then you can keep going."

I listened to everything she said, and while I didn't agree with it, I respected her enough to try to follow her wishes. At least until that didn't work and then we'd do things my way. Because I was sure as fuck that her way wouldn't work. "I won't hurt him, but I will make it clear that I'm watching him, and if he doesn't pull his head in, I'll be stepping in for you."

"Thank you," she said as she stood on her toes to kiss my cheek. "You're a good brother, Kick."

"We'll see if you still think that after he fucks up again and I lose my shit at him."

She shook her head. "You have so little faith in people."

"It's what happens when you've been fucked over by people too often, babe."

Her face grew wistful. "We need to find you someone to love. Someone who will love you so much you might start to believe in people again."

I ignored her and jerked my chin towards the front door. "Go. You don't want to be late."

She grinned at me and turned to walk away. "I'm going to start looking," she threw over her shoulder as she left the room.

I shook my head to myself as I went in search of the kids. When my sister got an idea in her head she never let it go. She could try all she liked but I'd never be like her. She was too fucking compassionate and forgave too easily.

There'd only been two people in my life who I'd ever thought I'd be able to forgive if needed.

Turned out me and forgiveness didn't get along well.

78

Chapter Seven

Evie

I slammed my front door and trudged down the hall. My efforts this afternoon to get hold of money for my father's debt had been for nothing. No one had been able to offer me a cent and I'd run out of people to ask. Dread snaked through me at the thought of what would happen to Dad if I couldn't find the cash for him.

The silence and heat of the house was suffocating. After spending the drive home completely in my own head, riddled with thoughts about my father, I needed music to drown them out. I dumped my bag on the kitchen counter and switched on the air conditioning and stereo before I headed to the shower. Maree would be here to pick me up in a couple of hours and I needed to clean the grime of the day off. I needed this night out tonight like I hadn't needed one in a long time.

***

Maree clinked her glass with mine and indicated for me to take a sip. "Here's to hot sex with Kick," she said, laughing.

I rolled my eyes. "I should never have told you," I muttered. But the conversation about Kick had put my worry about Dad out of mind, and that was what I needed tonight.

Her eyes twinkled with mischief. "You should totally have told me. I wanna meet this man who's got you all flustered."

I shifted on my stool. The humidity in the outdoor bar we were at had caused my long hair to stick to my neck. Thank god I'd worn a sleeveless dress tonight. Probably didn't help that the conversation about Kick was getting me all hot and bothered. I eyed Maree and decided to open up to her about Kick and my family. She'd only known me for two years and I hadn't shared much with her so far. I'd had enough alcohol tonight to spill my life story, though. "I've known Kick pretty much my whole life," I began.

Her eyes widened. "Wow."

"His family and mine lived on the same street and our mothers were best friends. Kick was a year older than me and always kept an eye out for me at school, made sure I was okay and wasn't being picked on."

"I'm guessing if someone picked on you, he came down on them."

I smiled. "Yeah, he did. Him and Jeremy. The three of us were inseparable." The memories swirled around me, causing butterflies in my stomach.

"So your families are best friends and you two grew up thinking you'd have a happy ever after together?" she asked, a tinge of hopefulness in her voice. Maree dreamt of happy ever afters.

She was so far from the truth. "No, our - "

A voice from behind cut me off. "No, my father fucked it all up when he fucked Evie's mother." The bitterness in Kick's voice could not be missed and I spun around in shock. I didn't realise he still felt that way about his father.

As I stared at him, Maree said, "Well, that would do it."

He tore his gaze from mine to look at her. "Yeah, it would."

I felt the need to put some perspective on it. "It takes two to tango, Kick. Your father wasn't the only one at fault."

His hard gaze met mine again. "Evie, your mother had just lost a *child,* for fuck's sake, her marriage was crumbling under the strain of that as well as your father's gambling, and she was in pain . . . My father knew she was vulnerable and he went after her knowing full well she wasn't in her right mind. Don't make excuses for him."

I took a long swig of my drink. These memories sucked, and I wanted the alcohol to blot them out.

Before I could say anything, Maree asked quietly, "Your mother lost a child?"

I nodded, sadness enveloping me. "Yeah, my sister, Shelly. . ." My voice cracked and I stopped talking. Shit, this never got any easier. Not even after nineteen years.

Because the guilt still tears me apart.

"Our families were on our yearly holiday that we took every summer when Shelly fell out of a tree," Kick explained, watching me carefully, his eyes full of concern.

All three of us sat in silence, lost in thought. Our fun night had quickly turned sombre. I stared at my glass, absently running my finger around the rim while Shelly occupied my mind. When I looked up, I found Kick watching me intently, his shoulders and body tense.

Eventually, he said, "I need a drink. Either of you want another one?"

Thank God.

We nodded, gave him our orders, and then sat watching him walk to the bar. My gaze shifted over his white t-shirt that loosely skimmed his muscles, and then moved down to the black jeans and motorcycle boots. I'd never known another man to wear sexy the way Kick did.

Maree cut into my thoughts. "Babe, he's hot. How the hell did you walk away from him? I don't know if I would ever let

81

him out of my bed if he was mine."

She was the best kind of friend a woman could have. Always able to read my needs, I knew she'd deliberately changed the subject. She'd known I didn't want to talk about my family shit anymore. I smiled at her and then winked. "I can tell you now, if Kick was yours, you definitely wouldn't want to let him out of your bed."

She grinned. "You're a dirty, dirty woman, Evie Bishop. But seriously, what happened between you two?"

I sighed and leant my elbows on the table. "We argued a lot. And on top of that, Kick's got a darker side he won't share with me. Like, he would just shut down and disappear for days at a time. I know he's trying to protect me but he's never understood that there's nothing he could do that would stop me from loving him. He's always been there for me, every single time I needed him, so I would always be there for him."

"So you still love him?"

"I never stopped loving him, but I walked away because there's no future for a couple where one of the partners won't give themself completely."

Her eyes twinkled again. "So a little sex on the side would be okay then."

I laughed, the alcohol in me softening my resolve a little. "It would be a bad idea."

"What would be a bad idea?" Kick asked as he placed our drinks on the table.

His voice slid right through me. When I met his gaze and found heat there, the alcohol buzzing through me collided with my desire for him and caused the kind of need no woman could deny. Against all my better judgements, I flirted with him. "Sleeping with you," I said.

He didn't skip a beat. "No, that would be the best fuckin'

idea you've had in a long time."

I cocked my head to the side. "You don't think it'd be a good idea for us to get to know each other again before we had sex?"

"Baby, you and I know each other better than we know anyone else." He moved so our faces were close and whispered, "Some days I think I know you better than I know myself."

The air whooshed out of me and I reached my hand out to the table. "I need a drink. Quick," I muttered, and once he'd passed it to me, I gulped half of it straight down. Placing it back on the table, I said, "How do you do that?"

"Do what?"

"That thing where you say something sweet that makes me want to forget everything we've been through and let you back in?"

"There's nothing sweet about me, Evie." His eyes flashed hardness for a moment before reverting back to the softer gaze he usually reserved for me.

"Not true. You just gave me sweet."

"No, I just gave you the truth. Don't mistake that for sweet," he said with the hard tone I knew so well. It was the tone he used whenever he was about to shut down on me.

"You two should totally get a room. Or maybe you should schedule a date for Valentine's Day and work your shit out," Maree said.

I answered her without taking my eyes off Kick. "He doesn't do Valentine's Day. Kick's not your hearts and flowers kind of man."

"She's right, but I do make sure my woman is satisfied in other ways on Valentine's Day," he said, eyes still on me, a promise held deep inside them.

As lust roared through me, I gulped the rest of my drink

down. When I'd drained the glass, I asked Kick, "Jesus, was that a double? It was strong."

"Yeah."

I raised my brows. "You trying to get me drunk?"

He smirked. "Don't need to. You've already taken care of that."

I decided I needed a moment away from him so I hopped off my stool. "I'm going to the ladies', Maree. You wanna come? Kick can look after our table."

"No, babe, you go. I'm gonna interrogate your man while you're gone."

I laughed. Maree was the queen of interrogation but what she didn't know was that Kick was the king of evasion. "Have fun, you two," I said and left them to it.

I wobbled my way to the ladies' room. Kick was right when he said I was drunk. Time to slow the drinks down or else tonight would go way past messy.

The line at the ladies' was long, and I started chatting with some of the women, so it took me twenty minutes to get back to the table. As I'd suspected, Kick must have evaded most of Maree's questions because she looked frustrated. "How did your interrogation go?" I asked her with a grin.

She poked her tongue at me. "You knew I'd have no luck, didn't you?"

"Totally, but who knew, maybe you would be the one to break him."

She stood and grabbed her bag off the table. "I'm done for the night, guys."

I frowned. "Really? I thought we'd catch a cab together."

"I got a call while you were gone." She grinned mischievously. "I've got a sure thing waiting at his house for me. Sorry, babe, but I can't pass him up, and Kick said he'd take you home."

Of course he did.

Smiling at her, I said, "Okay, go. I wouldn't expect you to give up a sure thing."

She blew me a kiss and turned and left. When I shifted my gaze from her to Kick, I found him watching me intently. "How did you know I'd be here tonight?" I asked.

He slid another drink across the table to me. "How do you know I didn't go to more than one place looking for you?"

God, he was killing me tonight. I drank some of the bourbon he'd gotten me. Shit, another double. When I placed the glass back down, I said, "How many did you go to?"

He didn't hold back. "Six."

Fuck.

I took another drink. "Why?"

"Why what?"

"Why now, Kick? Why all of a sudden do you want to try this again, and what makes you think it would be any different to the two times we already tried to make it work?"

He raked his fingers through his hair. "It's not all of a sudden for me, Evie. I've never stopped thinking of you, never stopped thinking I fucked it all up by letting you walk away. But I didn't want to fuck your life up any further so I stayed away. I think deep down I always thought we'd find each other again when we were older. Jeremy's death hit me hard and made me realise just how short life can be. I don't want to wait till we're older. I don't want to fuck around anymore."

I emptied my glass, taking a deep breath as the bourbon burnt on the way down. "Just because you don't want to fuck around anymore doesn't mean it would work. Not unless you've changed your idea of what being a couple is," I said softly.

85

He leant his face close to mine. So close I could almost taste him. "Let me in, baby. Let me show you how I've changed." Kick had never been the best at expressing his emotions but his eyes laid it all out for me.

Vulnerability, want and hope.

I placed my hand on his cheek.

One night wouldn't hurt.

Surely.

"Show me," I whispered.

Chapter Eight

Kick

19 years old

I pushed Evie against the wall and reached my hand under her dress to trace a pattern up her thigh. Her eyes fluttered shut for a moment and she moaned when my fingers found their way into her panties.

"Fuck, baby, you're wet," I growled as I dipped into her.

Her eyes opened and she threaded her arms around my neck, pulling my mouth to hers. Before she kissed me, she said, "I've been wet for you for years, Kick."

Eager lips met mine and when her tongue found mine, I grunted my approval and ground my dick against her while my fingers fucked her pussy.

When she ended the kiss, she said, with a lick of her lips and a fucking sexy smile, "Best birthday present ever."

Fuck, I needed in.

With my dick, not my fingers.

"How do you like to be fucked, baby?"

Hesitation flared in her eyes and she whispered, "I'm still a virgin, Kick."

Fuck me.

My eyes widened. "What the hell? You had a boyfriend all last year."

"I did but that doesn't mean I'm gonna give it up to just anyone."

She's going to give it to me.

I pressed my finger deeper inside her and picked up the pace. At the same time, my lips crashed down onto hers and I devoured her mouth, all the while pushing my erection against her.

I fucking need that pussy **now**.

She groaned and curled a leg around mine, trying to pull me closer. We couldn't get any fucking closer, but I knew what she craved because I craved it, too.

Skin.

I needed her skin against mine.

I pulled away from her and moved my hands to the bottom of her dress. In one swift movement, I had it up and over her head and on the floor. My gaze dropped to her tits, and fuck me if she didn't have the hottest fucking bra on I'd ever seen.

"You like it?" she asked.

I flicked my eyes to hers. "Like it? I fuckin' love it," I rasped as I reached around the back of her to undo it, "but it's gotta come off."

She hit me with that sexy goddamn smile of hers, moved her hands to the top of her panties as if she was about to remove them, and asked, "What about these?"

"Off," I commanded, eyes glued to her pussy, waiting for it to be revealed to me.

She pushed them down and flicked them aside. Without waiting another second, I knelt in front of her, placed my hands on the backs of her legs and ran them up until they cupped her ass. I pressed my mouth to her pussy and licked my tongue the length of her slit.

She tastes so fucking good.

One of her hands landed on my head and I vaguely heard her moan but it was like it was coming from a distance because, at that moment, I was lost to her cunt.

Lost to every-fucking-thing I'd dreamt of for years.

My tongue circled her clit before I pushed it inside her.

So goddamn wet.

I chased her orgasm with my tongue while my fingers dug into her ass. When I moved one of my hands around so I could work her clit, she shuddered and cried out my name.

I fucking loved the sound of my name crying out from her lips.

"Oh god . . . Kick . . . I'm gonna come . . ." Both her hands were in my hair now, pulling and pressing as if she needed me closer and then needed a break.

And then she came, and I experienced a feeling like I'd never experienced in my life.

Utter fucking happiness.

I was straight up and her hands went straight to my clothes, frantically tearing at them until they all lay in a heap on the floor.

Our eyes met, and greed shot through me like never before.

I grabbed her by the back of her neck and pulled her mouth to mine. "I fuckin' need your cunt, baby," I growled before roughly kissing her.

She hungrily kissed me back, and I pulled her with me to the bed.

"Lie down," I ordered, "I'm just gonna get a condom."

When I came back to her, she was spread out like fucking heaven on my bed. Her eyes searched mine and I saw vulnerability there. Positioning myself between her legs, I leant my face down and kissed her before pulling away and whispering, "I'll go slow and try not to hurt you."

Fuck, I'd never fucked a virgin before and I hoped to fucking God I wouldn't lose control and hurt her.

"I trust you, Kick," she said softly, her eyes gazing at me with all the trust in the world.

Once I had the condom on, I moved over her and she wrapped her legs around me. Keeping hold of her eyes while I did it, I slowly entered her.

Oh, fuck.
Feels so fucking good.
"You okay?" I whispered, our faces so close.

89

She nodded. "Yes."

Her hands slid around my neck and she pulled my face to hers so she could kiss me. Gentle at first, and then she kissed me harder.

I pushed my cock further in, still slowly, in an effort to not hurt her too much. A pained noise escaped her lips, though, and I pulled my mouth from hers to stare down at her with concern.

She gave me a small smile. "I'm okay, please keep going," she insisted.

I stilled. Searching her face, I asked, "Are you sure? I can stop if you want to."

Shaking her head, she pleaded, "No, I want this, Kick. Please don't stop."

Her eyes conveyed the truth in her words so I pushed all the way in.

Fuck me.

Amazing.

"Okay, baby, I'm gonna keep going," I said, giving her notice.

She smiled again and lifted her head to meet me with a kiss. Her arms wrapped around me and she held on tight, ready for this to happen.

I pulled out, and eyes still focused on Evie's, I pushed back in, all the way. But not hard. Not yet. Her eyes widened but she squeezed her legs tighter around me as if she was telling me to keep going. So I did. This time I pulled out and thrust in a little harder.

Fucking hell, Evie's pussy was tight. This could be over fast.

I pulled out again and thrust hard. My release teased the edges of my consciousness and I dropped my head into her neck as I continued to pump into her.

She moved her hips with me, and fuck, I was so fucking close. "I'm gonna come, Evie," I grunted through hard breaths, almost at the point where I wouldn't be able to hold back any longer.

She didn't say anything but just squeezed her legs around me tighter, her pussy squeezing tighter around my dick. I took it as another *sign to keep going and a minute later, I came. Harder than I'd ever come before.*

Once I'd wrung every drop from my orgasm, I lifted my head to look at her. She smiled up at me, and I apologised, "I'm sorry you didn't come."

"I did earlier so it's okay."

"No, it's not, but I promise the next time you will."

Surprise flared in her eyes. "Next time?"

I frowned. "You thought this was a once off?"

"I thought this was you showing up to help me celebrate my eighteenth and then taking me home for a one night stand."

"Fuck no," I said as I pulled out of her and pushed up off the bed to dispose of the condom. When I came back from the bathroom I brought a cloth with me to clean her up, but she'd pulled the sheet up to cover herself.

I sat on the bed next to her and frowned. "Why did you cover yourself?"

Her face flamed red. "You turned the light on."

"Yeah, cause I want to clean you up so I need to be able to see for that."

"Oh my God, Kick, I can clean myself up!" She seemed embarrassed and I couldn't figure out why.

"Evie, we just fucked . . . I just had my mouth on your pussy, and you're embarrassed for me to clean you up?"

She covered her face with her hand for a moment and then she sat up so our faces were level. "It was dark and you couldn't see my body," she whispered, her eyes reaching out to me, to understand.

And I did fucking understand, and it made me fucking angry.

I moved her hand, the one clutching the sheet to hide her body from me. When the sheet fell, I ran a finger across the top of her breasts. With my gaze fixed to hers, I said, "Don't let those bitches from school make you believe you're not beautiful. Just because they told you you're

91

ugly or whatever the fuck they told you, it doesn't make it true. And it's not fuckin' true, Evie." I leant my face down to whisper kisses over her breasts. When I'd finished, I said, "You're the most beautiful woman I know."

Tears threatened to fall, but she held them back. Swallowing hard, she said, "Thank you. I'm such an idiot for believing them." Her voice drifted off as she spoke so that the last few words were almost a whisper, and she hung her head.

I placed a finger underneath her chin and tilted her face up with it. "You're not an idiot, you've just had so much shit thrown at you that you've started to believe it."

As I sat and watched her take that in, my chest tightened. Evie had been through so much and yet she was the best person I knew. Even though people had been so mean to her, and nasty, she was still the kindest and most caring person in my life. And I'd been an idiot last year after I finished school. While she finished her final year, I'd joined Storm and focused all my attention there, neglecting our friendship.

I was fixing that mistake now because if I was truly honest with myself, I'd wanted Evie for years.

I wanted her in my life.

And in my bed.

***

I leant against the doorway of my bedroom and watched Evie sleep.

Peaceful.

Fuck, she was beautiful. I had a permanent fucking hard-on for her and, she had no idea. Not fucking her last night had been one of the toughest things I'd done in ages.

She stirred and a moment later her eyes came to mine. "Morning," she said, and then she winced, placing a hand to her head.

I pushed off from the wall and walked to her side of the bed. Sitting on the edge, I passed her the water on the bedside table and two aspirins.

"Thank you," she murmured, taking the pills from me. Once she'd swallowed them, she gave the glass back to me.

I stood and asked, "Do you have to work today?"

"Yeah."

"Okay, I'll take you home so you can get ready and then I'll take you to work. And then I'll pick you up after work."

"I can drive myself, Kick," she said, her voice off. I thought we'd made progress last night but uncertainty now hit my gut.

"No, you can't. You'll be over the limit."

She stared at me, in obvious pain from her headache, and I was sure she was about to argue with me again when she surprised the shit out of me and said, "Fine, you can drive me."

"Good, that's fuckin' settled. I'll wait for you in the kitchen."

I left her to it, and a moment later I heard her crashing around in my bedroom. Relief hit me, thank fuck she'd agreed to let me drive her because she was definitely in no state to be driving.

When she appeared in the kitchen ten minutes later, I took in her hung-over state and fuck if my dick didn't jerk again at the sight. This woman could make me want to fuck her even if she was dressed in a fucking sack and had a shaved head.

She's it for me.

I grabbed my keys off the table and jerked my chin towards the front door. "You ready to go?"

She nodded and slowly headed outside. I followed close behind, watching her ass sway in that sexy-as-fuck black dress she'd worn to the pub last night. She'd ripped it off as soon as we'd gotten back to my place and done her best to get me to fuck her, but I'd had no intention of sleeping with her. Not in that state. No, the first time we had sex again, we'd both be sober. I needed to know she wanted this as much as I did. And until I got her to that point, I wasn't laying a hand on her. As hard as that would fucking be.

***

I still hadn't decided what I was gonna do about Peter and Gambarro when I picked Evie up from work that afternoon. Seeing her, though, pushed me towards the decision of getting involved. How the fuck could I let her father die?

I drove her home and insisted on walking her inside so we could finish our conversation from the other night.

"Okay," she agreed, seemingly as keen to talk as I was.

Aside from the other night and this morning, I hadn't been in Evie's house for over a year. She lived about twenty minutes from me, in a small house she'd saved for years to buy. I clearly remembered the day I'd moved her in and we'd christened a few of the rooms. Back then, it had been in need of renovating and I'd helped her. It looked as if she'd done more since I'd been here last.

As we walked down the hall, I murmured, "I like what you've done with the place."

"You like the colours I've added?"

I smiled. "Yeah, baby, I like it." Evie loved colour and she'd painted feature walls throughout. Teal seemed to be her favourite colour these days, judging by the amount of it in her home.

We made it to the kitchen and she dropped her bag on the counter and looked up at me, seeming rather hesitant. "Why didn't you sleep with me last night? I thought you were all up for sex and then you fobbed me off."

That was unexpected, but I was more than happy to discuss it. "I am *all* for sex with you but not like that."

"What does that mean, Kick?" she asked me, clearly frustrated.

"It means you're worth more than a quick fuck to me. If I can't have you... have your heart, then I don't just want your body."

Silence surrounded us as she processed that. I waited patiently. She had to relent soon.

Finally, she said, "I need more. It's not enough for you to just show back up after all this time and say you've changed your mind."

"What do you need? Tell me and I'll give it to you."

"I need *all* of you."

My body stilled. She wanted the parts of me I didn't want to give. She wanted the parts of me that no one in their right mind would want to know.

The parts she would run from if I showed her.

"No, you don't."

She stepped nearer to me. Our bodies were so close I could feel her warm breath on my skin, and fuck, I needed more.

I needed to feel her body on mine, her hair between my fingers, her pussy around my dick.

Her words at the end of the day.

Her love wrapped around me, taking all the shit away.

"I've known you since I was seven, Kick. You used to share yourself with me back then. Your thoughts and feelings. And then, after all the shit went down with our families, you started to pull away and when you joined Storm, it was like you disconnected from me. I tried so hard to get through to you, to

95

let you know I loved you, *all of you*, but you never took that in. I get that there's stuff you can't tell me, and I don't want to know the ins and outs of it all, but give me something. Anything. Show me *you*. Let me love *you*."

Fuck.

I didn't deserve her. She was lightness to my darkness and I had no idea how to combine the two. Or even if I wanted to.

I reached out and ran my finger lightly down her cheek. "I love you, Evie, but I don't know how to do what you've asked. I can try, though," I whispered, total honesty spilling from my lips.

She smiled sadly at me, a look of defeat in her eyes. "I know."

When she moved away from me and just watched me in silence, I feared I'd fucked it all up.

I'm losing her again.

And then I did what I always did when fear and hopelessness threatened to overtake me - I resorted to anger and frustration. "This isn't the fuckin' end of this," I snapped, and stalked out of the room without waiting for her response.

I didn't need to see her rejection again.

I just needed to find a way to get through to her.

Chapter Nine

Evie

I hadn't heard from Kick in two days. Not since he told me he didn't know how to be in a relationship with me. My heart hurt and that pissed me off. Why did he have to show up and create these feelings when I was doing okay without him? And why did he struggle so much with letting me in? When we'd been together in the past, it was like Kick lived two lives. One with me, and one with his other family, the club. I could never work out why he kept the two completely separate. What kind of person doesn't want to introduce you to his friends? It made me feel like shit when he refused to let me meet them. I wouldn't put myself through that again.

I'd decided to try and put him out of my mind when I realised that would be impossible. Out of the question, actually, because when I visited my mother two days after he'd walked out of my house on an angry outburst, Kick was at her house again.

As I entered her kitchen, I asked, "Where is he? I saw his bike out front."

She looked up from the vegetables she was cutting up and smiled at me. "He's out the back, cleaning the gutters."

"Why?"

She frowned. "I guess because he's a nice guy and wanted to help me."

"So he just dropped by and decided to do it for you?" I asked, incredulous.

"He told me he'd noticed them the other day, so that's why he came back. Are you annoyed about it?"

I huffed out a breath. "I don't know how I feel, Mum. I'm like a big knot of stress at the moment. One minute I want him and then the next he pisses me off and I just want him to leave." God, I felt like one of those whiny bitches I couldn't fucking stand.

Just make up your mind already.

A huge smile spread across her face. "Baby, you've always loved Kick, and from what you just said, I don't think that love is going anywhere soon. You two have always had that push and pull where you piss each other off, so that's nothing new."

"Maybe I don't want a relationship like that anymore. Maybe I want something easier with no pissing each other off."

She laughed. "Oh, Evie . . . you'd be bored in a day."

She was right and I fucking knew it.

And that pissed me off even more.

God damn it.

I left her and went in search of Kick. I found him and Braden up on the roof out the back. He didn't realise I was there for a couple of minutes, so I took the opportunity to watch him and just soak him in. He was shirtless and his muscles rippled as he moved. And I had an awesome view of his ass, too, so every time he bent over, he blessed my eyes with that ass.

Oh god.

My mother was so right when she said I'd be bored without the push and pull Kick and I had.

I still love him.

With every fibre of my being.

With every scar he'd left on my heart.

I still want a life with him.

98

As I was caught up in my thoughts, he must have seen me. "Evie," his voice filtered through and I blinked him into focus.

"Hi," I said, smiling up at him.

"You staying long?" he asked, his frustration with me from the other day gone.

I had a couple of things to do, one of them being to visit my dad to get more information out of him about the guy he owed money to. I'd been desperately trying to find a way to borrow the money but I'd still had no luck yet so I figured maybe we could negotiate with the guy. "I've gotta go and see Dad but I'll be here for a while."

A look of irritation crossed his face, and he said, "I'll be down in a minute."

"Okay." I had no idea what the irritation was about but I figured he would clue me in soon.

"Hey, Evie," Braden called out, waving to me.

I waved back. "Hey, Braden. Long time, no see."

"Yeah. I reckon it's about time you two got your shit sorted," he said with a huge grin.

I waved him away with a flick of my hand. "Yeah, yeah... you wouldn't be the first person to say that."

He laughed a huge belly laugh. "Well get on that, woman."

I shook my head and laughed. "I'll leave you guys to it. I'm going back inside out of the heat."

"Have a coldie waiting for me," Braden said.

I smiled to myself. I'd missed the banter with Kick's brother. Although our parents had killed their relationship, us kids had stayed friends, but when Kick and I had broken up the last time, I'd cut all ties. I'd needed to put distance between us, and being friends with his family would make that hard.

As I turned to walk back inside, I caught a glimpse of Kick standing on the roof staring down at me. He seemed surprised

99

about something, and I couldn't figure out what, so I just gave him a smile and continued on.

My phone rang a second later and I answered it absently. "Hi," I said, having no idea who it was because I hadn't even checked the caller id.

"What's got you all distracted?" Maree asked.

Thank god. I could get her perspective on this before I saw Kick again. "Who do you think?"

"I am guessing it's that hot man of yours." I could practically hear her licking her lips.

"He's not my man. But fuck, I think I want him to be."

"Of course you do, babe. I mean, who wouldn't?"

I laughed. "No, Maree, I mean I really do want him. Not just for his body."

She grew serious. "As in, you still love him?"

I sighed. "I never stopped loving him. I just didn't want to admit it. But I don't know how we can make it work with all the baggage between us."

"If you want him, you have to fight for him. You have to work out what's holding you back and find a way to get rid of it. 'Cause I've gotta say, you're an amazing woman, Evie, but you came alive when you were with Kick the other night. I've never seen you light up like that. On your own, you kick ass, but I can only imagine how awesome you'd be with Kick by your side."

Shit.

I knew what it was.

It's funny how you can be searching for an answer for a long time and then someone says something and it's like the block is moved and you can see clearly.

Fuck.

It wasn't Kick after all.

It was me.

"I know what's holding me back."

"What?"

"Me."

"Huh?"

I sighed. It was so stupid I didn't even want to tell her. "After my mother slept with Kick's father and the shit hit the fan, everyone in the neighbourhood called her a slut and then they called me a slut. They said I was just like her. I was sixteen and had never even had sex, and yet they were spreading all these nasty rumours about me. The girls at school bullied me and I lost pretty much all my self-esteem. I never felt good enough. I never felt like anyone would want or choose to be my friend after that. So, when Kick chose not to introduce me to his friends when we were dating, all the insecurities I thought I'd put behind me flared up, and I felt like I wasn't good enough." I paused and ran my hand through my hair. "Shit, Maree, it was me all along. My stupid negative self talk that I didn't even realise. And I'm supposed to be a fucking counsellor."

"Oh, babe, don't beat yourself up about it. We all have hang-ups and blind spots. At least you've figured it out now," she reassured me.

"Yeah,' I murmured, and then said, "Shit, sorry, I hijacked the conversation. What did you ring for?"

"No worries, babe, I was just calling to see if you wanted to go out for a drink tonight?"

"I might pass. I've gotta sort some stuff out with my dad, and now I think I want to talk to Kick."

"Sounds like that might be a good idea."

"I'll call you and let you know how it goes," I promised, and we hung up.

A noise came from behind me and I spun around to find Kick

standing there, his intense gaze on me.

"You still love me?" he asked gruffly. His shoulders were rigid and his breathing shallow while he waited for my answer.

My heart beat faster in my chest and my tummy fluttered. "You heard all that?" I whispered.

He nodded. "Yeah, baby, but answer me. Do you still love me?" The fierceness in his voice turned me on and made me want to crawl into his arms and beg him to be mine forever.

"Yes," I said, finally admitting out loud what I had been denying for so long.

He took that in but didn't say anything else for what felt like ages, and then he shoved his fingers through his hair, messing it up more than it already was. The energy between us vibrated with want and the frustration we'd both been feeling for too long. And then he stepped into my space. One arm slid around my waist and his other reached up to cup my cheek. He brushed his thumb over my lips in the way he'd always liked to do, and he murmured, "I've always loved you and you've *always* been good enough. Fuck, *I'm* the one who's not good enough." He stopped talking for a minute and his eyes left mine to look down at my lips. When he returned his gaze to mine, he said, "I wish you'd told me how it made you feel. I didn't keep you out of that part of my life because you weren't good enough. I did it because I didn't want to drag you into that shit." He bent his face closer to mine so our lips were almost touching, and my core clenched at the closeness. "You're too good for it, baby," he whispered.

I pressed myself into him and wrapped my arms around his body, loving that my hands were on him again, after having denied myself his touch for so long. A growl rumbled up from his chest and heat flashed in his eyes. And then we both moved at the same time.

Our lips met and it was like everything was right in my world again. This was exactly where I was meant to be in this moment.

With Kick.

The man I'd loved as a boy when he used to let me ride his bike because I didn't have one.

The man I'd loved as a teenager when he took on the mean girls for me, and wiped my tears away when I didn't feel good enough.

The man I'd loved at eighteen when I gave him my virginity and he treasured that for what it was.

The man I still loved for so many reasons, but mostly because he *got* me. He knew all my hopes, fears and flaws, and loved me regardless.

My mouth parted and his tongue slid in.

Possessive.

Demanding.

Loving.

I moaned and his arm around my waist tightened, and he pulled me closer, pushing his erection into me. Lust shot through me and I knew this was it.

This was the moment I was giving myself back to him.

Kick was mine.

I was Kick's.

He ended the kiss and leant his forehead against mine. "Fuck, Evie... you've got no idea what you fuckin' do to me." He lifted his head so he could look me in the eyes. "You give me hope I can be a better man, that I'm not just the sum of all the bad shit I've done in my life."

I frowned. "You're not a bad person, Kick."

He closed his eyes for a moment and when he opened them again, the desolation I saw there pierced my heart. "Yeah, I am, baby," he whispered, cracking my heart a little more.

I opened my mouth to argue with him some more, but his phone rang and interrupted us.

He pulled it out and checked who it was. "Sorry, I've gotta get this," he said with regret, and walked away from me to take the call.

I waited for him to return, doing my best to recover from our kiss and my realisations. He wasn't gone long, but when he came back to me, the Kick who'd been with me a minute ago was gone, and in his place was the guy who looked at me through hard eyes. This was the Kick I didn't know so well but so desperately wanted to know and understand.

"I've got something I've gotta take care of," he said, his voice as hard as his eyes.

"Will you be back?"

"I don't know, but Braden will finish the gutters."

"I'm not worried about the gutters, Kick. What I want to know is when will I see you again? We were kind of in the middle of something there."

"I'll call you," he said, and I felt like I was being dismissed.

What the hell?

He'd already started to leave before I could get my wits together and challenge him. However, he stopped and turned back to me. "Don't go to see your father. I'm gonna sort that out, okay?"

"What the hell is going on?" I demanded, growing more frustrated.

His hard look intensified and he stalked back to me. "Promise me you won't go to your father, that you won't try to fix his shit for him. I went to see him and I told him I would help him with it."

I stared at him in shock. A minute ago he'd been telling me

104

he loved me and now he was talking to me as if none of that had been said.

"Promise me, Evie," he barked.

I jumped, and was instantly pissed off. "You better go and sort your shit out, Kick, and *then* you'd better come find me and explain to me what the fuck is going on! Because something has happened here that I don't know about, and I'll be damned if I'll put up with this shit."

His eyes bore into mine for another moment and then he nodded. "I'll see you later," he promised, and turned and left.

I stood completely stunned and didn't hear Braden come up behind me. "He needs you, you know."

I jumped again and turned to face him. "Fuck, Braden..." I muttered.

He held his hands up. "Sorry, didn't mean to frighten you."

"What do you mean, he needs me?"

"I don't know exactly what shit Kick's involved in with his club, but he's struggling. Actually, I think he's drowning in it, whatever it is. He doesn't spend much time with us anymore and when we do see him, he's this moody, angry fuck who none of us really want to be around."

"Really? 'Cause he hasn't really been that moody with me."

"See? He needs you because you take it away for him. He's never stopped loving you, Evie. He hasn't even dated anyone since you two broke up."

"I never knew that," I said, surprised again. God, today was a day of discovery.

"Give him a chance. But know that it might take some time for him to change his ways. Yeah?"

It was almost as if he was pleading with me. Braden was a big guy. Way over six feet and built with muscles that looked like they took hours in the gym to achieve. He stood in front of me, his dark, wavy hair sweaty from being outside, his muscles tensed and a demanding look on his face, telling me he how much he wanted me to do what he asked. But it was his eyes that said the most. They gazed at me through pain; Braden was hurting from watching Kick struggle. Nodding, I said, "I don't intend to give up on him, but he's gonna have to step up, too."

He smiled. "I'll give him a kick up the ass for you."

It seemed like Kick might need more than that. I just hoped he had it in him to be the man I needed him to be.

Chapter Ten

Kick

I strode into the clubhouse, looking for Hyde. The motherfucker had called and demanded I get down here straight away. Right when I was finally starting to get my shit together with Evie. Pulling me away from my woman had not fucking pleased me, and I was about to give him a piece of my mind.

"Kick!"

I spun around to find Hyde coming up behind me, a hard glare in place. Walking towards him, I asked, "What the fuck is going on, Hyde? What was so fuckin' important that I had to get here right fuckin' now?"

"Did you go and see Jonathon Gambarro?"

"No."

He narrowed his eyes. "You sure about that, Kick?"

"Yes, I'm fuckin' sure about that, motherfucker. Why?"

"Well, it seems someone from Black Deeds got in his face and he's gone fucking psycho on them, so I wanted to make sure you weren't thinking of taking him on. I told you, the last thing we need is a problem with Gambarro."

He wasn't fucking serious? "You dragged me all the way here when I was in the middle of something to tell me *that?*"

I watched his eyes flash with rage. "It'd pay for you to remember who you're talking to," he said, his fury rising fast.

"I never forget who I'm talking to, VP. And you know my loyalty to this club, so don't come in here and insinuate that I am anything but fuckin' loyal." I shook my head in anger. "The shit I've done for you, for King and for Storm, go above and fuckin' beyond. If you ever imply it hasn't or doesn't again, you might just find out what it's like to be on the end of my anger."

"Are you fucking threatening me?"

I moved closer to him so we were almost nose-to-nose, my anger rolling off me. "Yeah, I'm fuckin' threatening you."

Hyde looked like he wanted to punch me, and I had no doubt the thought was running through his head, but I could fucking care less. If he wanted a fight, I'd give him a fight. In the end, though, he turned and stalked out of the room.

Fuck.

I was between a rock and a fucking hard place. And I still had no idea what the fuck I was going to do about it.

***

Five hours later, after I'd gone for a long ride to blow the shit out of my head, I pulled my bike up in Evie's driveway. Her lights were still on, and I wondered if she'd waited up for me. She'd been pretty fucking clear about me coming over so my guess was she had.

As I walked the short path to her front door, she pulled it open and stood staring at me.

Christ, she never failed to take my breath away. Tonight she was dressed in an old t-shirt of mine that I didn't even realise she still had. Her long, brown hair was flowing wildly around her shoulders and her face was flushed.

"Sorry I'm so late," I apologised.

"Better late than never," she replied quietly.

I waited for her to step aside and let me in but she didn't. "You gonna let me in?"

"Not until you spill."

I exhaled harshly. "Evie…"

She crossed her arms over her chest and a determined look covered her face. "No, Kick. I need you to tell me what happened today. I want to know where you go when The Hard Kick comes out."

"Come again, babe? What's The Hard Kick?" She'd lost me now.

"It's this thing you do every now and then. One minute you're okay and normal, and then something happens and you change. It's like a harder, meaner version of you comes out. And it's not that I don't like it, I just want to understand why. Is it something I do to you?"

There were three steps separating us. I closed the distance and curled my hand around her waist. Leaning in to bring our faces closer, I said, "No, it's not something you do. It's got nothing to do with you at all."

"But - "

I pressed my finger to her lips. "I'm sorry it happens. I've got shit going on with the club at the moment and as much as I try to keep that from interfering with us, I can't always manage to do that."

Her face softened and I sensed her relenting. "I get it. But you do need to explain to me about my father and what you're doing to help him."

"We'll get to that, baby, but fuck, I haven't been able to stop thinking about you all night, so can we deal with that first?"

Heat flashed in her eyes. She didn't say anything, just nodded her agreement.

I moved my free hand down to the bottom of her t-shirt and trailed my fingers up her thigh towards her panties. When her eyes fluttered and she bit her lip, I knew this was what she wanted, too. I pressed my mouth to her ear and murmured, "Let me inside, Evie. I need to fuck you like I've never needed to fuck you." I found the edge of her panties and pushed past them to run my finger along her pussy.

So goddamn wet.

She whimpered, and unable to control myself any longer, I moved quickly and scooped her up. I entered the house, kicked the door shut behind me and strode towards her bedroom.

Her hands came around my neck and she held on tight. "I've been thinking about you, too," she breathed into my ear, causing my already hard dick to nearly lose his shit.

I deposited her on the bed and then reached down to undo my belt and jeans as I kicked my boots off. She moved off the bed and came to me, lifting her t-shirt over her head as she did so. Her hands went to my tee and she had it off in a matter of seconds. My jeans and boxers followed close behind.

Her eyes travelled every inch of my body before coming back to meet my gaze. "God, Kick, how much do you work out these days?"

I pulled her to me, fucking loving the feel of our skin together again. "It's called working my frustrations out. I haven't had you to work out with for too fuckin' long so I had to find another outlet."

She raised her brows. "You can't tell me you haven't been working out with someone else."

"Every now and then, but babe, none of them come close to you."

"Yeah, yeah…"

She tried to blow me off but I corrected her. "No, Evie. You know I don't say shit for the sake of saying it."

Her body stilled in my arms and I knew I'd gotten through. Her hand came to my face and she caressed my cheek. "I know," she whispered.

My cock throbbed for her, it fucking ached to get inside her, so I hurried this along. "I'm gonna fuck you hard and fast to start with and then long and slow. You good with that?"

A sexy smile spread across her face. "So long as I get your tongue on my pussy later, I'm good with anything."

Christ, I loved her dirty mouth. Had missed that mouth. "I see your mouth is still as filthy as it's always been," I said as I let her go and pushed her back onto the bed.

"Kick, you taught me everything I know, so of course my mouth is filthy as fuck."

"Fuck, Evie," I growled as I positioned myself over her. "I'm gonna fuck your mouth with my cock later and show you just what filthy is."

She reached for my dick and began stroking it. "I don't want you to use a condom. Are you clean?"

"Yeah. You?"

She nodded and then caught my lips in a kiss while she continued to pump my cock. I knew I was dangerously close to coming and that I should slow this down, but I couldn't bring myself to do it. She made me feel so damn good and I hadn't felt good in a long fucking time.

Her touch was magic.

Her words were healing.

And I knew her love was everything I needed in this shitty world.

I pulled out of our kiss and grunted, "Babe, either you need to stop what you're doing or I need to get inside you because I'm just about to blow if you keep it up."

She let me go but said, "You did say this was gonna be hard and fast and I'm good with that."

"I don't want it to be *that* fast. I don't think you realise what

111

you do to me. These days I just need to look at you and I'm almost coming in my pants."

"Baby, you sure know how to sweet-talk a girl," she whispered in my ear.

I groaned. Even the feel of her warm breath on me almost did me in. Fuck, I was so far gone it wasn't fucking funny.

It was time to take control.

I grabbed both her wrists and positioned them above her head. Holding them there with one hand, I held her gaze and said, "Don't move your hands."

"Why?"

"Because if you touch me, I'm gonna come all over you instead of inside of you."

"That wouldn't be so bad," she teased.

"Christ, woman, don't fucking tempt me."

"Okay, I'll just lie here and let you do whatever you want."

"Thank fuck," I muttered and let her hands go, half expecting her to move them, but she didn't.

Now that I had her whole body to devour, I began with her neck and then trailed my tongue down to her breasts. Evie had the best tits I'd ever had the pleasure of touching. Even after all her weight loss, they were a good handful, and I wasn't in the minority in my devotion to them. I'd had the displeasure of watching men ogle them for too many years now. As I sucked and licked them, she arched her back and moaned. I paused for a moment to look up at her face and almost lost control when I saw the bliss written across her face. Her eyes were shut, and her teeth were biting her lip. My woman was sexy as fuck.

Her eyes fluttered open and she found my gaze. Smiling lazily at me, she murmured, "You should keep going, baby. I want you to lick all the way down to my pussy and then I want you to fuck me with your tongue."

I leant on my elbows, my face resting in between her tits. "That right?"

"Yeah. You think you can manage that?"

I moved quick and a second later, I'd straddled her and had dipped my face to hers. My dick sat at her entrance and I teased her with it, pushing slightly into her and then pulling out. "I can manage any-fuckin'-thing, darlin'. The question is, can you?"

She licked her lips and asked, "Like what, Kick?"

I pushed my dick inside again. Not all the way, just enough to get her going, and then I pulled back out. "Like that," I growled in her ear, "can you manage that?"

She smiled that fucking sexy smile that made my dick even harder than it already was if that was even fucking possible. "I don't think you want to push me, Kick, cause we both know I can take a lot more than you can. I'd only have to reach down, take your cock in my hand and give you a few tugs and you'd be coming before you could say fuck."

Fuck.

I was done.

Between her sexy body, her wet pussy, and her filthy mouth, my senses were in overdrive to the point where I could hardly function.

I thrust inside her, all the fucking way, and then pulled back out and slammed back in again. Stilling with my dick still deep in her, I rasped, "Feel good, baby?"

Her arms reached around me, and she dug her nails into my back. And then she squeezed her cunt around my dick and said, "Feels real good. Keep going."

Fuck me.

I'd missed this woman.

I pulled out and thrust back in.

Over and over.

113

She clung to me, her nails clawing my back, and her mouth chanting filthy words that turned me way the fuck on.

And as my orgasm built, I knew she was it for me. In that moment, I knew I never wanted to fuck another woman in my life. All I needed to be happy was Evie's beautiful pussy wrapped around my cock, and her heart to belong only to me.

"Fuck, Kick, I'm gonna come!" she screamed, and I thrust harder and faster.

"Wait for me, baby," I grunted as I chased it.

She held on tight and together we came. I pumped my cum into her as her pussy pulsed around my dick and took everything I had to give.

I nestled my face into her neck and rested there while we both recovered from our orgasms. Eventually, I lifted my head and kissed her before saying, "Fuck, that was good."

"Yeah, it was," she agreed. Then she smacked my ass and said, "I'm gonna go clean up and then you can start that all over again."

I grinned and moved off her. "You do that. We've got a lot of time to make up for."

"We do," she agreed, and then left me to go to the bathroom.

I shifted onto my back and placed my arm behind my neck while I waited for her.

Shit, how the hell did I get so lucky?

To have Evie back in my life made me the happiest fucker on the planet.

I wasn't going to fuck this up again.

And it was clear to me now what my next move was.

And where my loyalty now lay.

***

The next morning, I sat on the edge of Evie's bed and did my boots up, getting ready to tackle the shit I had to take care of during the day.

She rolled over and the bed shifted as she sat up. I turned to look at her and found disappointment in her eyes. "What?" I asked, confused.

"Are you leaving now?"

"Yeah."

She sat up straighter and moved the sheet to cover herself which only confused me more. I moved my hand to the sheet to pull it back down. "Don't," she murmured, holding the sheet tight.

I shifted so I was facing her with one leg up on the bed. "What's going on? Why the fuck are you covering yourself up after last night?"

"What is this, Kick?"

Now I was really fucking confused. "What do you mean? I thought we knew what this is."

She motioned toward me with her hand and said, "Why are you dressed and leaving so early? It's like you're running out on me."

I flicked my hand out to catch hers. "This," I pointed to myself with my other hand, "is me fighting for you, Evie. Fighting for us. This is me bringing you into my world."

She sucked in a breath but didn't say anything, just waited for me to go on.

I struggled with where to begin. "I've done a lot of shit in my life I'm not proud of." I let go of her hand but she reached for it and grabbed hold of me. My gaze dropped to our hands and then shifted back to her. The fierce look of love on her face gave me what I needed to continue. "I've hurt people, for fuck's sake." She needed to know this, but it fucking sucked to have to

115

lay it all out, because I knew she'd probably want to walk away from me once she knew it all.

"Okay." She said nothing else, just sat quietly waiting for me. Like that wasn't enough for her to make up her mind.

"How can you love a man who does that?" I demanded, needing more of a reaction from her. I couldn't gauge her thoughts from a simple 'okay'.

She shifted closer to me on the bed when she should have been shifting further away. "Kick, you forget I've known you for almost your whole life." She placed her hand on my chest. Over my heart. "I know you *here*. I know the good you carry in you, and I know you feel like you have no good left in you, but I see it. I see *you*. So when you tell me you've hurt people, I know you would have had your reasons. I don't judge you." Her gaze never left mine as she gave me those words and I saw no judgement there, only acceptance.

I stared at her, stunned into silence for a moment. "Storm is involved in a lot of shit and I'm buried deep in that shit, baby. I'm not gonna spell it out for you, but it's not fuckin' legal shit. Can you handle that?"

She blinked a few times, giving away her hesitation, and I waited for the blow to come. "I'm not an idiot. I've always figured the club was into that kind of stuff."

"And you don't care?"

"I wouldn't say that. I'll admit it concerns me, but I put it out of my mind."

I scrubbed my face. "Shit, Evie, if we're together and I bring you into this world, there are gonna be things you won't be able to put out of your mind."

"Like what?"

"Like the shit that's about to go down with your father."

She sucked in a breath. "What's about to go down with my

116

father?"

"He owes all that money to a fuckin' dangerous man who wouldn't hesitate to kill for an unpaid debt. I'm gonna blackmail the guy into letting your dad out of his debt. And that shit will probably blow back onto the club, and fuck knows where that will end up."

Worry took over her face, and I hated that I'd put it there, but she wanted the truth. And then she gave me something - my first glimpse of hope that we might have a future together. "So Storm is into shit and some of it I won't be able to put out of my mind, but I know that you're the kind of man who protects what is his. And if I'm yours, I know deep in my soul that you'll do anything to make sure I'm safe. That's how I know I'll be able to handle this shit."

Her words took my breath away.

She accepted this.

Me.

She accepts me.

I roughly pulled her to me and wrapped her in my arms. "Fuck, you amaze me," I murmured as I held her close, never wanting to let her go.

When I did eventually release her, she smiled and said, "Together, Kick. We'll get through anything if we just stick together. We always have."

I stood. It was time to go and save her father.

Bending, I kissed the top of her head and said, "Happy Valentine's Day, baby."

I ignored the look of surprise on her face at my words.

Yeah, I never used to celebrate Valentine's Day.

I could change, though.

I could change for Evie.

***

"Mr Gambarro isn't taking visitors today."

Was she shitting me? I eyed the woman who was blocking my access. Uptight, middle-aged bitch who probably just needed a good fuck. "I don't give a flying fuck if he's not taking visitors. You tell him I'm here to settle a debt, and that he's gonna want to see me." I paused and then added, "Tell him it's about Michael."

She scowled. "I'm not interrupting him. You'll need to make an appointment like everyone else."

I slammed my hand down on her desk, causing her to jump in her seat. "Go and fucking tell him I want to see him and that it's about Michael!" I roared.

She glared at me and continued to argue. "I don't know who Michael is - "

Rage blinded me and I struggled with my kneejerk reaction to inflict pain in order to get what I wanted. Instead, I placed both hands on her desk and bent my face close to hers. "Bitch, I'm about two seconds away from doing some major damage here. Go and tell your boss he's got a fuckin' visitor."

Her eyes widened, and then she stood and walked into Gambarro's office. A minute later, they both came out, and Jonathon Gambarro glared at me. I eyed him and took in one of the most feared men in Sydney. He'd had his hand in dirty shit for over twenty years, and at only forty-one I figured he had many more years of it left in him.

"Who the fuck are you?" he barked.

"I'm here to settle Peter Bishop's debt."

He scowled. "Why isn't Peter here to take care of that?"

I walked towards him and threw out the one weapon I had in my arsenal. "I've actually come to talk more about Michael than

118

about Peter."

The asshole knew exactly who I was talking about by the look that flitted across his face.

I'd brought fear to Jonathon Gambarro. A feat not many managed to do. And I hoped like hell it would be enough to save Peter.

He motioned for me to enter his office.

Time to negotiate.

Shutting the door behind him, a more subdued Gambarro took a seat at this desk while I stood on the other side. "What about Michael?" he asked as his gaze swept over me with distaste.

"What do *you* think, asshole?"

"I'm not sure what to think unless you lay it all out for me." His voice remained calm but the sweat beading on his forehead gave him away.

I slowly placed my hands on the edge of his desk and bent slightly towards him. "It seems you've got a thing for young boys, Jonathon, and I happen to know one of them didn't make it out of your home alive. That information remains with me, and me only, as long as you wipe Peter's debt and forget you ever met him. And before your brain starts to tick over and contemplate ways to take me or Peter out for this, you need to know I've made arrangements for this information to be passed onto the cops if either of us end up dead."

He weighed my words, and I watched the hatred form in his eyes. "How the fuck do you know about this?" he sneered.

"Knowing shit that no one else knows is my specialty."

"That shit is likely to get you killed one day. You do realise that, don't you?"

"I'm not concerned about that. I've lasted seventeen years in this shithole city with the knowledge I have. I don't think anything's about to change just because I've got something on you."

His brows shot up. "Well, then you've got no fucking idea how I work."

I bent lower to look him right in the eyes. "No, motherfucker, *you've* got no idea how *I* fuckin' work. You don't want to take me on because I've got reach in this city that you can only fuckin' dream of."

"I don't even fucking know who you are, so excuse me if I don't buy a word of what you're saying."

Time to pull out the big guns. I started rattling off names he *would* know. "Justin Sutherland, Billy Jones, Max James, Eric Bones, Calvin Ryan, Stu Davy... you know any of those names? And I promise you that's just the tip of the iceberg. You wanna fuck with me, you'll be fucking with them, too." I intentionally left out King's name just like I'd intentionally not worn my cut this morning.

He sat back in his chair and I knew I had him.

Silence filled the room as we glared at each other, and while he contemplated his next move.

I should have felt anxiety, worry, concern . . . anything.

I felt nothing.

Years of doing this shit for King had numbed me.

My job was to get the shit on people, throw that shit at them and sit back and watch them crap their pants. It was to bend them to our way of thinking, and I was the fuckin' best at it. It was why King kept me so close. He knew I had good contacts, and he knew the cold heart beating in my chest meant nothing was off the table when it came to getting what we wanted.

If Gambarro didn't come to the party now, I had other options to force him. But it seemed the first option I'd gone with would be enough.

120

He pushed his chair back and stood. When he spoke, his voice was low. Cold and calm. "Consider the debt wiped."

I nodded once but didn't say anything. He had more to get off his chest and I knew it.

"Also consider this a warning. I don't like the way you conduct business and I intend on showing you just how much it displeases me. And I don't care how long it takes me to do that, be it months or years, I *will* see it through. Now get the fuck out of my office," he said in a low, menacing voice.

With my goal achieved and nothing else left to say, I turned and walked out of his office. I knew he'd make good on his threat so my next stop was the clubhouse. It wouldn't take Gambarro long to figure out I was Storm, so I had to let King know what had just gone down.

While I figured Hyde would be pissed, I suspected King would rally the boys. The crazy motherfucker lived for shit like this.

***

It took me nearly an hour in traffic to get to the clubhouse and, in that time, word had travelled. Gambarro was on the warpath. He hadn't worked out my connection to Storm yet but Hyde had already heard about what had gone down.

Hyde found me before I found King. Anger rolled off him. I'd never seen him this fired up. "What the *fuck* did you do?"

"I sorted some family shit out," I threw back at him. "Just like you would have done if it was your family on the line."

"No, what you did was create club shit and that's something I sure as fuck wouldn't have done. When Gambarro figures out who you are and that you're with Storm, he'll come, gunning for us, and he won't fucking hold back. I can promise you that."

"You don't think I've already thought of that?"

"I seriously don't know what the fuck goes through your mind anymore, Kick. If I didn't know better, I'd say you had a head full of pussy and had lost your fucking mind, but seems as though I know you're a cold-hearted bastard who doesn't ever let pussy control him, I don't know what's gotten into you."

"Hyde," King's voice sounded from behind me and as he got closer, he said, "we're backing Kick on this."

Hyde's anger and frustration grew and he channelled it into a punch to the wall closest to him. "Fuck!" he roared as he stood staring at us, his eyes wild, his face flushed. "Do you know what the fuck that will do to Storm, King?"

King was the master of controlling his emotions when he wanted to and he did that now. The vein pulsing in his neck was the only giveaway he was angry. "Of course I fucking know what this will do to Storm. I also know we have the connections to take him on. And win." He turned to look at me, his eyes flashing from anger to that wicked look he got when something excited him. "And I'm in the mood for some fun. Let's shake this shit up, boys. Let's show Sydney what the fuck Storm is made of."

Hyde shook his head. "Fuck, you're an insane motherfucker sometimes, King."

King grinned. "It keeps life interesting, my friend."

"And what about this other shit with Silver Hell? If they figure out that was you, then we'll have two lots of assholes coming after us," Hyde said.

King shrugged. "Bring it on. Like I said, Storm is connected, and if need be, I'll fucking drag our other chapters in."

Hyde raised his hands. "I've had my say. You're the President, so whatever you say goes, but I'm letting you know I

122

think this is some fucked-up shit."

King took in what he'd said and then grew serious. "Hyde, we're brothers. If one of us needs help, we all pull together. Kick *always* has our backs. It's time we take his."

Hyde stared at both of us for a long moment and then blew out his breath. "Fuck," he muttered. "Yeah." And then he walked away, leaving King and I alone.

"Thanks, brother," I said.

"No thanks needed. Whatever you need from me, you have it. Just ask."

I nodded and watched as he, too, walked away.

Storm had become my family when my own had fallen apart years ago and King had always been there for me. He'd just shown me I was true family to him because King never offered anyone whatever they needed. He never told anyone just to *ask* for what they needed. Usually you had to sell your soul to get that kind of offer from King.

Fuck.

I'd sold my soul a long fucking time ago.

King was only giving me what I was due.

Chapter Eleven

Evie

I shimmied into the new red dress I'd bought today and smoothed it down into place. Stepping in front of the mirror in my bedroom, I assessed myself. Not bad. I'd spent the day pampering myself with a haircut and colour, and then a pedicure and wax. Kick might not be the kind of man to celebrate Valentine's Day, but that didn't stop me from acknowledging it and looking good for him. Tonight, I planned on seducing him into giving me multiple orgasms. Kick was the only guy I'd ever slept with who'd been able to do that for me, and I could hardly wait to get him started. Shit, I'd been thinking about it all day and was more than ready to go, so the first one wouldn't take him long.

Once I was happy with my dress, I headed into the kitchen. It was nearly seven o'clock. Surely he'd be here soon. I'd actually expected to see him much earlier today but he must have had a lot to take care of because I hadn't seen or heard from him since he left my bed this morning.

I kept myself busy for another half hour but when I still hadn't heard from him, I decided to call him instead.

He didn't answer.

Shit, where was he?

I sat at the kitchen table and thought about it for a few minutes, and then I knew. Well, I had an idea of where he might have gone so I grabbed my car keys and went in search of him.

Fifteen minutes later, I walked into the pub that used to be 'ours'. It was the place he took me to celebrate my eighteenth birthday, which then led to us getting together, so I'd always thought of it as ours.

He was sitting at a table in the far back corner. Alone, and he wore a look that told me he was contemplating stuff. Something bad must have gone down. It was never a good sign when Kick was contemplative.

I walked to where he sat and he looked up as I approached. His eyes were vacant - it was as if he was looking straight through me. And then he blinked and I must have come into focus for him, because his gaze travelled over my body. When his eyes came back to mine, I saw the want in them that had been missing a minute ago.

"Evie," he murmured, "what are you doing here?"

I sat opposite him, hating that he'd asked me that. "Is it not okay that I came looking for you?"

He reached his hand across the table to take hold of mine. "It's always okay for you to come looking for me."

"So why did you just ask me what I was doing here?"

"Guilt," he said softly and didn't elaborate.

"What's wrong, Kick?"

He stared at me for what felt like ages. He seemed to be weighing something up and I expected something bad to come out of his mouth but he surprised me when he finally spoke. "I fucked up Valentine's Day."

"Why?"

"I should have picked you up earlier and taken you on a date. I'd planned to . . ."

"I think we both know dates on Valentine's Day are not your kind of thing, and I'm okay with that."

"Yeah?"

I smiled. "Yeah. But you're gonna have to make up for that in other ways."

Heat flared in his eyes. "I think I'm good for that, baby. I don't think I could fuck that up even if I tried."

"I think you're right there. You have mad talents in that department."

He laughed, and it was so damn good to see him relax a little. "Good to know my talents are appreciated," he said, letting go of my hand and sitting back in his chair.

My smile faded. "Now, are you gonna tell me what's really going on, because I am betting it's got absolutely nothing to do with Valentine's Day? Is it something to do with my father? Is that why you're sitting alone in this pub tonight looking like you're assessing your whole damn life?"

"This is our pub, Evie. It's where I come to think."

Warmth spread out from my belly.

He remembers.

"Yeah, I know it's our pub," I said, and then asked, "What are you thinking about?"

"Do you ever look back on your life and wonder if you could have done it better?" His eyes watched me intently, waiting for my answer.

I nodded. "Yeah, I do it a lot." I drove myself crazy with my thoughts sometimes.

He listened to what I said, remaining still. His body was so tightly wound by the looks of it and I wanted to lay my hands on him and try to work some of that tension out. But what Kick needed at this very minute was a listening ear so I gave him that instead.

Eventually, he stretched his arm back to grab hold of the back of his neck, letting out a muttered, "Fuck," while he did it.

126

I leant my forearms on the table and shifted forward in my seat. "Please tell me what's wrong."

"I sorted your father's debt today . . . but I've caused other problems in order to do that."

My relief was short-lived as what he'd just said filtered through. I frowned. "What kind of problems do you mean?" My heart beat faster in my chest at the thought something bad would come of all this.

He reached for the beer in front of him and took a swig before placing it back on the table and absently running his finger around the rim. Eventually, he gave me his eyes, and said, "It's nothing the club and I can't handle, but . . . fuck, I don't know, have you ever gotten to a point in your life where you feel sick of all the shit you have to deal with? Like, if you'd made different choices in your life, things would be so much different."

"Yes," I whispered, not taking my eyes off him.

"I just want this to be simple, Evie," he said quietly.

"What?" I asked, unsure of what he was referring to.

Anguish burned in his eyes. "Us. I just want us to be easy for once."

My heart squeezed in my chest.

I hated seeing him hurt.

Standing, I held out my hand to him. His brows pulled together, questioning, so I said, "I want it to be easy too, Kick, so I'm going to show you how much I love you, and we're going to make a pact to stick together no matter what. Life might be hard, but you and I can do everything possible to make *us* easy."

He stared at my hand for what felt like ages and then gave me his as he slowly stood. When his gaze met mine, he said, "I fuckin' hope so, baby."

127

"Stop," Kick growled, his arm wrapping around my waist and pulling me back to him as he came through my front door. He closed the door behind him and whispered in my ear, "That was the longest fuckin' ride."

I let my head fall back on his shoulder, and when his mouth found my neck a moment later, I moaned as his lips set my body on fire. My hand reached up and my fingers slid through his hair. Gripping tight, I admitted, "The last three years have been the longest fucking years, Kick."

He ground his erection against my ass. "Fuck, baby, never going there again," he promised gruffly. His mouth pressed harder into my neck, and his lips and tongue worked their magic on me. His hand skimmed up my body, ghosting over my breasts and my neck to eventually end up in my hair. My core nearly exploded when he roughly grabbed my hair, yanked my head to the side, and rasped, "You ready for your Valentine's present?"

Fuck.

I'd missed this.

Missed Kick's rough side.

Before I managed to form coherent words, his hand that was around my waist, reached down to the bottom of my dress, and pulled it up high enough to give him access to my panties. His hand slid straight in, his fingers gliding through the wetness I'd had for him all day. He teased me for a few moments, sampling my pussy without giving me what I wanted. What he *knew* I wanted. Every time his finger came near my entrance, I pushed myself into his hand, trying desperately to force him inside, but he quickly moved his finger away and circled back to my clit.

"Kick . . ." I groaned, trying to move my head out of his hold so I could attempt to gain some control back.

"No," he growled, holding my hair tighter, yanking it harder to the side, showing me who held the control here. His finger ran circles over my clit again before slowly moving back down. "Tell me how much you want this, baby," he ordered, his finger hovering over my entrance, teasing the hell out of me again.

"I want it so bad," I mewled, my mind and body completely consumed with the need for his finger to be inside me.

"I'm not convinced."

His gravelly voice drifted into my consciousness, and I decided to show him rather than tell him. I moved one of my hands down to his with the intent of making him do what I wanted, but his hand swiftly left my panties to grab hold of mine. A groan escaped my lips at being thwarted.

"I said tell me, not show me," he warned, trapping my hand in his firm grip.

Lust had taken over my body, pure need flowing through every vein. Kick had always been a master of bringing me to the edge, of driving me to complete desperation.

Desperate for his touch.

Desperate for his words.

Desperate to be joined as one.

"I want you more than anything else in this world, baby," I whispered.

He stilled and I waited.

I knew those words would send him over the edge, and I was right. He let me go so he could roughly push me against the wall. Forcing his body hard against mine, his hands took hold of my face and his mouth pressed down onto mine as he took what he wanted. A searing kiss that was as demanding as it was tender.

My arms wrapped around him and I dug my fingers into his back, knowing that would fire him up as much as my words had.

Kick was right about something he'd said the other day — we knew each other so well. Sex with him was amazing because we knew exactly what turned each other on.

His kiss grew more urgent, his body pressed even harder against me, and I took everything he had to give. Years of denying our desire shaped this kiss and I felt it all.

He devoured me.

He worshipped me.

He loved me.

"Fuck, you're beautiful," he murmured as he ended the kiss and searched my face. His finger lightly traced patterns over my lips. When he forced my lips open, I took what he offered and sucked his finger, tasting myself there, swirling my tongue over his finger because I knew he loved that. I knew he got off on me tasting myself and loving it.

I reached for the button on his jeans and he let me, but he never took his eyes off mine. Once I had his jeans undone, I reached in and took hold of his hard cock, running my thumb over the pre-cum on the tip. His eyes fluttered shut for a moment and he exhaled a hard breath. When he gave me back his gaze, I said, "I'm ready for your Valentine's present now."

"Suck my cock, baby . . . show me how fuckin' much you love me," he commanded, heat-filled eyes telling me how much he wanted that.

My lips pulled up at the ends in a smile. I loved sucking his cock. Without hesitation, I knelt and pulled his jeans and boxers down to free his cock. After he'd kicked his pants aside, I ran my hands up his legs, taking my time so I could appreciate the muscles he'd built since last I'd had this pleasure. His hand landed on my head. The way he held tight combined with the sounds of his heavy breaths told me how much he wanted this. I took hold of his cock and wrapped my lips around the tip and gently sucked it. Only the tip. Two could play at the game of tease.

His hand pressed harder on my head, trying to force me to take his entire length into my mouth. "Fuck, Evie, suck the whole fuckin' thing, baby," he groaned, obviously craving what I wanted to make him work for.

I gripped him harder and stroked the length of him while moving my mouth away. "All in good time," I murmured, enjoying the game.

Just as I was settling in to play with him a bit more, hands reached under my arms and yanked me up and over his shoulder. He strode down my hall and towards my bedroom while I cried out, "Kick! Put me down!"

His hand met my ass in a slap that jolted pain through me while at the same time causing intense pleasure to shoot through me. "Not fuckin' likely, sweetheart. You wanna play with me? Well, we play my fuckin' way," he said, and I almost came just from his words. At his promise.

Fuck me, I loved it when Kick took charge like this.

A minute later he dumped me on the bed before standing at the end of the bed and demanding, "Where are they?"

I shifted to lean on my elbows and look up at him. Frowning, I asked, "Where's what?"

"The cuffs I bought you."

Oh god, yes.

"In the bottom drawer," I said, pointing my chin at the chest of drawers in the corner.

He stalked over to the drawers, found what he was after and came back to me. "Up and turn around," he barked, indicating for me to stand in front of him facing the other way.

Without hesitation, I did what he said and a moment later, he snapped the handcuffs on my wrists and locked them into place.

131

His hand slid around my waist to spin me around to face him again. The carnal desire written on his face pulsed happiness through me and my body buzzed with expectation.

This is going to blow my fucking mind.

He ran his finger across my lips and said, "I want these lips around my cock and I want you to suck until I come like I haven't come in three fuckin' years." He paused, his gaze locked on my lips as if his mind was far away, and then he murmured, "There are no lips like yours, Evie."

As my body tried to cope with the assault of desire his words caused, his hands moved to my shoulders and pushed me down to my knees. Once he had me where he wanted me, one of his hands held my head in place while the other one guided his cock into my mouth. I took it all the way in and began sucking. My hands locked behind my back itched to be involved, but he'd made sure I had no control over this so I worked with what I had. My lips and tongue worked him up into a frenzy and I almost gagged as he forced his dick as far down my throat as he could, but Kick and I had this down to a fine art from years of practice and he knew when to back off and I knew when to breathe.

Kick's breathing grew ragged and he began grunting his appreciation of my mouth, and then he stilled and demanded, "You wanna swallow, baby?"

Still with his cock in my mouth, I nodded and he muttered, "Fuck." A moment later he pumped cum down my throat and I happily swallowed it all.

He pulled out and dropped to his knees in front of me. Reaching behind me, he undid the handcuffs and freed my hands before roughly taking my dress and bra off. He then moved his hand down to my panties and ripped them off. I shivered at his rough touch. So hot, and it turned me on even more. His finger found my clit and began massaging it. Then he slid his finger along my slit before finally . . . god, *finally*, pushing his finger all the way in. And then he fucked me hard with his fingers.

My body had been pushed to the edge of desire and I felt like I might collapse as he worked me up to my release. Kick sensed it, though, and put his free arm around my waist to hold me up. His mouth dropped to mine and he kissed me roughly before pulling away and saying, "I've fuckin' missed this pussy."

I shuddered as my orgasm built. Any minute now and Kick would have waves of extreme pleasure coursing through my body. "Don't stop," I managed to get out before the first wave hit.

He kissed me hard again, and said, "No plans to stop, sweetheart. I'm gonna make you come all night long. It's fuckin' Valentine's Day, after all."

My mind flashed with white light as the orgasm ripped through my body. My brain shut down as I let it take over me. I was sure Kick was whispering dirty words in my ear but I couldn't make them out. The only thing I could concentrate on was the fact he really was blowing my mind with his fingers.

I rode the waves and when I finally came to, I let myself fall against Kick who held me tight and then lifted me up and placed me on the bed. He positioned himself on the bed next to me and let his hand trail over my breasts. His eyes dropped to look at them and after he'd bent to take a nipple in his mouth and lightly bite it, he gave me his gaze, and rasped, "I need to get my cock in between these and fuck them."

Holy shit, he wasn't kidding when he said he had plans for the whole night.

My eyes followed his hands as he lifted his t-shirt over his head to reveal the hard muscles of his chest and abs. Oh god, a girl could get into trouble because of those muscles.

I shifted so I could catch his lips in a kiss and then said, "First you need to take care of my pussy and then you can do whatever the fuck you want."

He grinned at me and said, "I can manage that, but babe, not until you make me a promise."

"What?" I asked, ready to give him anything he wanted as long as he gave me his goddamn cock.

He roughly grabbed my face and pulled me back for another kiss. When he ended it, he bit my lip. Not too hard, just the way he knew I liked it. "Promise me you'll never lose that fuckin' dirty mouth of yours."

I grinned back at him and threw one of my legs over him before swiftly moving so I was straddling him. Arching my back and giving him an eyeful of tit in the process, I promised, "Yeah, baby, I promise."

His eyes had already been coaxed to my breasts and he reached up to grab hold of one.

Hell yes.

No fucking way was I letting go of Kick again.

Ever.

***

The next day, Kick came with me to see my father. To tell him his debt had been settled.

He answered the door with a look of surprise and we followed him into his kitchen. "You want a drink?" he asked, watching us warily. His gaze followed Kick's arm as it came around my waist and pulled me close.

Kick shook his head to a drink and I said, "No thanks, Dad. We've come to talk about your debt."

134

He pulled a teaspoon from the drawer and as he shovelled coffee into a mug, he pointed it at us and asked, "You two back together?"

Before coming here, I'd asked Kick to let me do most of the talking, and he kept quiet now and let me answer. "Yeah, we are."

A scowl crossed his face. "You sure that's for the best, Evie?"

His words angered me, and my body tensed, ready for a showdown if necessary. "I don't think it's any of your business. Not after all these years where you couldn't care less about me."

Kick's hold of me tightened and I heard his muttered, "Fuck." He didn't say anything else, though, and that impressed me. The Kick of three years ago would have been straight into an argument and fight if necessary.

Dad continued to make his coffee, remaining silent for a moment. Eventually, he stopped what he was doing, and asked, "Do you know what Kick's involved in these days?"

The look on his face told me he didn't think I did. "If you're referring to Storm, yes I know he's part of the club."

Dad's gaze flicked to Kick and the look he gave him was pure hostility. Then he looked back at me and said, "No, I mean the fact he bails me out of situations that involve thugs and criminals you don't ever want to be tied up with. I don't want you involved in that kind of stuff, Evie."

My blood boiled and I stepped forward. Kick loosened his hold on me but refused to let me go completely. "If you didn't want me involved in that shit, Dad, *you* should have stayed away from them. I do know what he's done for you and I also know that because of you, he could be in trouble now. That shit's on *you*, not *him*," I snapped, my eyes blazing the anger I couldn't control even if I tried.

He was taken aback, obviously not expecting me to fire up

135

like that, but memories of too many years of being let down by this man rushed at me now.

Kick finally waded into the conversation. "Evie and I are together now, Peter, whether anyone else likes it or not. And as far as her knowing what I'm involved in for you, I haven't told her the half of it, but I'm more than happy to if you'd like me to." I couldn't see his face but I could feel the fury in his voice and the hard set of his stance against my back.

Dad stared at him in silence for a few moments before turning his stare to me. "I'm sorry for dragging you into it." The room swirled with his regret. "I'm a weak man and I've let you down."

"Oh my god, Dad, yes, you're a weak man, but if you want to change your life, the only person who can do that is you!" Frustration at his excuses cut through me. He'd been full of excuses as long as I'd been old enough to understand what one was. "Stop making your pathetic excuses and man up. Yes, Mum cheated on you and your life went to shit after that. And yes, you lost a child . . . we all did, but we've all found a way to cope with that and live our lives . . . it's time you did, too. Find the good in your life and put the bad behind you."

Kick, who had little patience, got straight to the point of our visit. "Gambarro's wiped your debt, but so help me if you fuckin' get yourself into anymore debt, Peter . . . That was the last time I'm stepping in for you." His hand pressed hard against my waist and I knew in my soul that if Dad ever found himself in debt again, Kick would bail him out. Because he loved me, he would do anything for my family, or me, regardless of the words he'd just spoken.

"Thank you," Dad said, struggling to meet Kick's eyes.

"Did you see that counsellor I found for you?" I asked.

He hesitated and I knew if he said yes, he'd be lying. "Not

yet," he admitted softly, now avoiding my eyes.

Kick's frustration sounded in the long breath he pushed out. "Jesus," he muttered.

I pushed him. "When will you be seeing him?"

Cagey eyes darted back and forth between Kick and me before finally settling on me. "I'll call him soon."

My handbag had slipped down my arm, and I pushed it back up before saying, "Okay, you do that," I snapped, way past angry at his failure to help himself, "and don't call me until you have seen him. If you can't be bothered to sort yourself out, I can't be bothered to help you anymore."

Before he could say anything, I turned and stalked out of his house. Heartbreak, anger and disappointment sat heavy in my gut, and I swallowed the lump in my throat and fought back the tears threatening to fall. It killed me to give up on him, but I couldn't keep going the way we had been for most of my life. My father needed tough love now. I thought he'd hit rock bottom, but, obviously, he hadn't. I shuddered to think what that would look like when it finally happened because he'd looked pretty bad the last time I'd seen him.

Kick followed me out and when we reached his bike, he pulled me into his arms and kissed my forehead. "You okay, baby?"

I pulled back a little so I could look in his eyes. Those beautiful eyes that blared his love for me. It had been there all along but I'd been too blind to see it. I smiled. "Yeah, because I have you."

He planted a kiss on my lips and then said, "You've always had me, you just didn't know it."

My tummy fluttered and my heart expanded with happiness.

Even with all the sadness, grief, hurt and anger hanging over me, Kick helped take some of it away.

He gave me hope life could be good again.

Chapter Twelve

Kick

"Anyone else got anything to discuss?" King asked, casting his gaze around the room.

Church had been quick today, but we hadn't discussed the one thing I thought we would have.

And then Hyde stepped in. "Where are we at with Gambarro, Kick?" he asked, his steely eyes boring into mine.

I sat forward. I'd been ready for this. "As far as I know, he still doesn't know who I am. I've asked my contacts if they've heard anything and there's nothing on the radar."

"Gambarro's not a fucking idiot, Kick," Hyde asserted, "he'll figure it out soon enough and we need to have a fucking plan to deal with this shit."

King interrupted. "Our plan is what it's always been."

Hyde gave him an incredulous look. "What? Sit and wait for the shit to land at our feet and then defend ourselves?"

King's hard eyes narrowed at Hyde. "You think it would be better to announce to Gambarro it was us?" he asked scathingly.

Hyde shoved his chair back and stood. Shoving his hand through his dark hair, he bit out, "Fuck, King, I don't know what the fuck we should do, but I hate sitting here waiting. Like a sitting fucking duck." He glared at me. "We shouldn't be in this fucking position."

Devil, who only spoke when he felt it absolutely necessary, said, "Sit the fuck down, Hyde, and get your shit together, man."

I eyed Devil and he gave me a nod. He approved of what I'd done. I'd never hear those words from his lips, but Devil's actions always said everything you needed to know.

Hyde now turned his filthy stare to Devil. "Clearly, I'm the only one here who *does* have his shit together. I can't fucking believe none of you are worried about this."

Nitro sat next to me, his body tense, and his mouth firmly closed. No love was lost between him and Hyde, and I knew if he got into a heated discussion now, the fists would likely come out. Nitro was a smart man and extremely disciplined at keeping his mouth shut where Hyde was concerned, but today he lost the fight to contain himself. Cold eyes pierced Hyde and his voice was deathly calm when he spoke. "Clearly you're the only one who is forgetting Kick's loyalty to Storm. He's done shit for us that no man should ever have to fucking do, and he does it without a fucking word of complaint. I think you need to step the fuck back, pull your fucking head in, and shut the fuck up."

King smashed his fist down on the bench and stood, fury circling him. "Enough!" he roared. Pointing at Hyde, he yelled, "Sit down, Hyde, and don't say another fucking word." He watched as Hyde followed his orders, and then he turned to face everyone. "We're not fucking announcing anything to the world. Everyone is to keep their ear out and if you hear anything, you bring it to me. We clear?"

I looked around the table and found everyone nodding their agreement. Hyde nodded but his body language screamed his resistance.

"Right, that's settled. Anything else?" King asked, a look of impatience plastered across his face. He glanced around the table and when no one spoke, he brought the gavel down to signal we were done.

Hyde stormed out, and I watched King as his gaze followed Hyde. He'd always had a close relationship with his Vice President, but Hyde seemed to be causing him headaches lately. He eventually tore his eyes from Hyde and looked at me. "Don't worry about Hyde. I'll take care of him," he said, mistaking my concern for something it wasn't.

I shook my head. "I'm more concerned for you, Prez," I admitted.

A frown creased his forehead. "Why?"

"Your VP doesn't have your back and he's the one who's supposed to have it more than anyone else."

He processed that silently. "Yeah," he muttered, deep in thought. "He'll fucking have it soon enough, brother," he added, before stalking out of the room.

King could be persuasive, but I feared Hyde was in one of his moods at the moment and when Hyde was in a mood, nothing could get through to him.

Fuck.

***

Kick
17 years old

I placed the joint between my lips and inhaled its magic. The magic that would help numb me and make me forget, for even just a few hours, the shit I had to deal with at home. I sucked it deep into my lungs and held it there for a long while before slowly exhaling and letting my head drop back against the wall. I passed the joint to Jeremy and heard him take a hit.

When he was done, he passed it back to me and stretched out on his back on the floor. It was three o'clock in the morning and his house was silent as his family slept. We'd just gotten back from a lame party. He turned to look at me. "That party was shit."

I nodded. "Yeah, not one chick worth scoring."

He laughed. "That's one way to gauge it."

My brows rose. "How else would you gauge it, dude?"

"The lack of alcohol there, for one."

"Well, there is that, too, but I could have lived with that if there had been at least one hot chick, but there wasn't even that."

He turned silent and I moved my head from the wall to see what he was doing. Jeremy had been off all week and tonight his mood had shifted into something else again and I struggled to pick it. "What's up, man? You've been acting strange all week."

His body tensed but then he sat up and stared at me. The light from outside splashed across the room and I could make out the strain on his face and the rigid set of his shoulders. "Do you have secrets, Kick?" he asked, his voice heavy with burden.

"Jesus, man, we all have secrets. What the fuck's going on?"

The moment stretched before us, long and deathly silent. Whatever the hell he had on his mind was eating him up. I'd never seen Jeremy so troubled. Usually, he was the kind of guy who was confident and not fearful of anything.

Finally, he spoke. "I'm gay."

I stared at my best friend, taking in the torment he obviously felt over this revelation and hating that he felt that way. Hating that society made him feel that way. "I know," I said softly.

His eyes widened but he didn't say anything.

"I've known you for six years, dude, and for half of that time I've figured you were gay." I shrugged. "So?"

Anger clouded his face. "So? Do you have any idea how fucking big this is?"

"It's not big to me. Like, if you thought it would affect our

142

friendship, it won't."

He sat and stared at me, and I couldn't work out the thoughts running through his mind. When he eventually blew out a long breath, he said, "Fuck, I never knew you knew."

I took another long drag of the joint and then passed it to him. After I blew out the smoke, I asked, "Did you really think I wouldn't support you?"

"I didn't know, but I should have."

"Yeah, man, you should have. I've always had your back and I always fucking will."

"Shit, Kick . . . yeah, I know."

I eyed him, curious about something. "Does Evie know?"

He shook his head. "No, you're the only person I've told."

"You should tell her. She won't care, either."

"Thank you," he said quietly, his hands fidgeting after he passed me back the joint.

"What for?"

"For always being there for me. You've never let me down," he said, his voice uneven and his eyes showing me how much this shit was affecting him.

"Well, for the record, if anyone gives you any fucking grief over this, they'll have me to deal with. So you like to suck cock. Who the fuck gives a shit?"

He stared at me in shock for a minute and then he grinned and shook his head. "Fuck, Kick . . ."

"It's true, dude, and I'm okay with that, but don't ever fucking ask me to suck your dick, 'cause it's never gonna fucking happen. I'm all for pussy."

"I wish I'd told you sooner."

I nodded. "Yeah, me too, 'cause I've been wondering. You got any fucking idea how hard it is to think about your best friend being gay without thinking about cock? Thank fuck cock will never have to enter

143

my mind again." He laughed and I muttered, "Not funny, man. This is serious shit right here."

"So you don't want to come to a gay club and help me find a man when we turn eighteen?"

I slid back against the wall and closed my eyes. "Fuck, you know I can never say no to you. You and fucking Evie . . . always talking me into doing shit I don't want to do."

My eyes were shut, sleepy, but I heard his laugh.

Thank god we'd finally had that conversation.

I really didn't want to have to think about cock anymore.

***

That night, I knocked on Evie's front door and reached my arms up to grip onto the doorframe, stretching the tension out of my back. It'd been a long fucking day and she was all I'd been thinking about for hours.

She answered the door and my dick instantly jerked. I stepped forward, my arm circling her waist and sliding down to grip her ass. "That outfit is dangerous, baby," I growled into her ear. She had on the skimpiest denim shorts that were really just a scrap of material rather than a pair of shorts, and a tiny, fitted red singlet that stretched across tits that were straining to escape it.

Moving into my space, she put her arms around me, and said, "I'm hoping so."

I raised my brows and smirked. "Oh, really?"

She smiled. "Really."

"A man might need to be fed if he's expected to exert some energy," I said, still smirking.

"Might he?" She played with me and I fucking liked it.

"Well, you could try not feeding me, but I doubt you'll get

144

much out of me. My woman drained most of my energy last night."

A grin decorated her gorgeous face, and I loved that I'd put it there. "Okay, it's a good thing I cooked extra. I was hoping you'd come over," she said, grabbing my hand and walking towards the kitchen.

I let her lead me, my eyes never leaving her ass. "Sweetheart, I don't want you going out in those shorts. They hardly cover your ass, and I don't need to be dealing with motherfuckers checking you out, 'cause that shit could lead to me ending up in jail."

She turned and rolled her eyes at me. "No one will be checking me out except for you."

I yanked her hand so that she was propelled backwards into my arms. She stumbled but I caught her. When I had her eyes, I said, "Where the fuck do you get the idea that no one would be checking you out, 'cause last I looked, you're a fuckin' beautiful woman?"

Her face softened for a moment and she said, "Thank you," but I wasn't buying her belief in my words.

"You've got no idea, have you?"

"What? That you think I'm beautiful?" She seemed genuinely confused at my question.

"No, that every fuckin' man finds you beautiful."

Her mind hesitated to let her heart believe me; I saw it in her eyes. "Kick . . ." Her voice trailed off and she tried to move out of my hold, but I didn't let her. No fucking way was she getting out of hearing this.

"Sweetheart, I've been watching assholes eye fuck you for years. Those curves of yours were any man's fuckin' dream, and while I'm not a fan of this skin and bones thing you've got going on at the moment, you're still any man's dream."

145

Her mouth fell open and she stared at me with wide eyes. "You liked my curves?" The uncertainty in her voice fucking killed me.

"Fuck yes."

A smile slowly spread across her face, and I knew she'd heard me, and hoped she would start working on bringing the curves back. When she stood on her toes to give me the kind of kiss a man can only hope for at the end of a hard day, I knew I was in for a good fucking night.

When she ended the kiss, I slapped her on the ass, and said, "How about some food, woman?"

She grinned at me, grabbed my hand and led me to the kitchen.

A moment later, I stood in front of a banquet of food. "You made all this?" I asked, surveying all the dishes.

She placed plates on the counter for us. "Yeah, I know how much you love my Thai food so I spent the afternoon making it for you."

I crossed my arms and leant my hip against the counter. "And what if I hadn't shown? That's a fuckload of food, baby."

She gave me her sexy grin. "Oh, I was pretty sure you'd show."

I raised a brow, amused and way the fuck turned on at her confidence. "Really?"

A laugh escaped her lips and fuck me, I had to control the urge to close the distance between us and take her right now. She came to me, though, and I knew dinner was gonna go cold. She moved right into my space, laced her hands around my neck and pressed herself against my erection. "Really. You're a man who can't get enough pussy ever, and you seem to like mine, so I figured what I gave you this morning wouldn't be enough and that you'd be back for more."

I placed my hands on her ass and gripped her hard. She had no chance of escaping me now even if she wanted to. Bending my mouth to her ear, I growled, "Baby, I don't just fuckin' *like* your pussy. On a scale of one to ten, it rates off the charts. If you were the only woman alive, I'd kill every motherfucker to make sure you only had eyes for me." I shifted my face so I could look her in the eyes. "And Evie, it's not just your pussy I love." I placed my hand over her heart, and whispered, "I love what's in here."

She stared at me, the playfulness gone from her eyes. Her arm reached up and she gently laid her hand against my cheek. "I love you, Kick Hanson."

Fuck, I was an idiot to walk away from her three years ago. She had everything I'd ever wanted, but I'd let Jeremy convince me I wasn't good enough for her. That my world would only bring her harm. In this moment, I knew deep in my bones that I would *never* let any harm come to her. I'd fight to the bitter end to ensure her safety.

I lifted her and placed her on the counter. Stepping in between her legs, I brought my hand up to her singlet and skimmed my fingers over her breasts. A moment later, I had her singlet and bra off, and a mouthful of tit. My dick was so damn hard for her and I barely stopped myself from ripping the rest of her clothes off and banging her on the kitchen floor.

She arched her back, pushing her tit harder against my mouth, and I groaned. I grabbed her hair and pulled her head back. Lifting my mouth from her breast, I trailed kisses up her neck until I reached her mouth. Lightly biting her lip, I asked, "Are we gonna need the cuffs again or are you gonna play fair?"

Her legs wrapped around me as she promised, "I'll play fair tonight."

I let go of her hair and put my arms around her so I could lift her off the counter and carry her into the bedroom. After I let her down, I asked, "How many orgasms do you want tonight, baby?"

Eagerness flashed in her eyes and her hands went to her pants to undo them. "Just keep going until I pass out," she said as she pushed her shorts down.

I undid my jeans as I watched her remove her panties. Fuck, I was almost fucking panting like a horny teenager. She did that to me. I couldn't even wait. I reached for my dick and gave it a tug while never taking my eyes off her pussy.

She came closer to me and removed all my clothes while I kept stroking myself. Her scent intoxicated me, sending me closer to the edge. Her first orgasm was gonna come soon because I couldn't delay this any longer. I had to get my dick in her.

I scooped her up and a moment later I had her under me on the bed. Reaching down to her pussy, I got her started with my fingers.

Her hands reached for my face and pulled me down for a kiss. "Fuck, Kick, can we just start with your dick and skip the fingers?" she begged after she let my mouth go.

How the fuck did I get so lucky?

I did as she asked and thrust my cock in. "Never say I don't fuckin' do as I'm asked," I grunted as I pulled out and slammed back into her.

Hard, because she fucking loved it hard.

She held on tight as I relentlessly chased our orgasms. Her eyes closed and her mouth parted slightly as she took it all. I didn't move my gaze from her face; watching her unravel with pleasure had to be one of my favourite things to do.

As my release built, her pussy squeezed around my dick and she cried out my name as she came.

148

Fuck.

I kept at it until it hit me as well, and I gave one last hard thrust before coming inside her. My eyes closed as the orgasm exploded through me. It was the orgasm of motherfucking orgasms.

Evie did that to me.

I finally reopened my eyes and found her staring at me with a sexy gaze; a well fucking sated gaze. Shifting so I was beside her on the bed with a leg slung over her, I said, "One down and more to go, but I'm gonna need that food you made me first."

She moved onto her side and ran her hand along my leg that was now lying over her legs. Her hand made it to my ass where it lingered for a few moments before she ran it all the way up my side to my face. Smiling at me, she said, "I think that deserves a reward."

"Too fuckin' right that deserves a reward. Fuck, I think it also deserves a blow job later."

She licked her lips. "You have the best ideas, baby," she said as she moved off the bed. "I'm going to clean up and then I'll meet you in the kitchen."

Again I wondered, how the hell did I get so damn lucky?

***

We ate dinner and had just finished cleaning up when I leant against the counter and watched Evie finish packing up the leftovers to put in the fridge. The meal she'd cooked had been amazing but she'd always been a good cook so that had never been in doubt. She covered the last dish with tin foil and as she walked to the fridge she caught me watching her and flashed me a smile. Tilting her head, she asked, "What's going through your mind? You look deep in thought."

149

I wrestled with my decision whether to tell her or not. I'd actually been struggling with this decision for a few days and I'd come to the conclusion that for Evie and I to move forward, I had to tell her.

"It was Jeremy," I started and then stopped, trying hard to get the words out right.

She frowned as she put the last dish in the fridge. Shutting the door, she came to me and asked, "What was Jeremy?"

Shit, I had to get this out right because I didn't want her to end up hating him. I raked my fingers through my hair. "The reason I ended things with you. Jeremy convinced me that letting you get close to Storm would put you in danger, so I pulled away."

She stared at me, shock evident on her face. "What? I don't understand . . . why would he do that when he knew all I wanted was to be with you?"

Fuck.

I reached out and grabbed her hand, pulling her close. "Because he loved you as much as I do. Because he was the best friend either of us had, and he didn't want you to get hurt from your involvement with the club. Don't hate him, baby. He only wanted the best for you."

Wide eyes looked up at me, and the pain I saw there gutted me.

Maybe I shouldn't have told her.

When she burst into tears, I wrapped her in my arms and pulled her close.

Her body shook with sobs and I pressed my lips to her forehead, trying to soothe her.

We stayed wrapped together for a long time, allowing the memories to come and the grief to flow through us. I fucking missed him, and I wondered if this shit would ever get easier.

Not having him in my life had been hard but at least I'd always known he was close if I needed him. Now, he was fucking unreachable and that left a hole that would never be filled by anyone ever again. Not even Evie.

Eventually she pulled away and looked up at me through tear-soaked lashes. "I don't hate him. I never could . . . I'm glad you told me, because it changes the way I feel about how we ended things."

My brows pulled together. "How?"

She sucked in a breath and gave me a hesitant glance. "I thought you didn't love me enough to fight for me, but now I can see you loved me so much that you walked away with unselfish motives. You're such a good man, Kick, and you don't even realise it."

Her words washed over me like a soothing shot of love. They weren't accurate words but I fucking needed them and let a sliver of them in. I let them wash away some of the grime that covered my heart.

"Fuck, all that wasted time," I muttered.

Her eyes searched mine. "What made you change your mind after all this time?" she asked softly.

Moment of truth. I didn't want to, but I had to speak honestly even if it hurt her. I'd decided that being completely open with her was the only way we'd survive this harsh world together. "You've got no clue how hard it was for me to stay away all these years. When you shut me out completely a year ago, it nearly fuckin' destroyed me, baby. I've done a lot of things I never thought I would since then, not giving one shit about anything, because the only thing worth giving a shit about was lost to me. Some days I wake up disgusted with the person I've allowed myself to become. When Jeremy got in touch with me a couple of months ago, he told me he thought he was wrong. He said he'd watched you lose yourself over the last year and that he knew you and I should be together regardless of the club."

"Why didn't you come to me then?" I hated the sadness in her voice. She was right, though. I should have fixed this back then.

I looked at her with the regret that weighed me down. "I wasn't convinced he was right. The person I'd become wasn't someone I wanted you to know . . . but when he died . . . fuck, that fucked with my mind, Evie. I replayed everything over and over in my mind a million times, and then when I saw you at the funeral, I knew I had no choice." I paused and gave her a small smile. "My mind had no choice because my heart had already made it."

I'd barely gotten the words out when her arms came up around my neck and her mouth took over mine in a kiss I'd have paid all the money I had in the world for. It was a kiss that told me I'd made the right decision to be open with her and that I'd made the absolute right choice to fight for her.

It was a kiss that sealed my future.

Evie would be mine forever.

I'd make damn sure of it.

Chapter Thirteen

Evie

I cracked an eye open and squinted to read the bedside clock. Seven A.M.

Shit, it was too early to be awake on a Saturday morning. I closed my eyes, intent on getting at least another two hours of sleep. Kick had other ideas. His hand curled around my waist and made its way to my breast.

His warm breath coasted over my neck a moment later when he murmured in my ear, "Morning, sweetheart."

When his hand left my breast and started moving lower, I grabbed it and halted its progress. "No fucking way, Kick," I muttered, "you fucked me raw last night, and I can't even contemplate your hand or your dick anywhere near me today."

He chuckled and rolled onto his back. "Well, fuck me," he said, "you've never said no to me. Ever."

I rolled over to face him and raised my brows. "That's probably because you've never worked me like you did last night." I nodded in the direction of his crotch. "That dick of yours has worn my pussy out and she needs a break today. And my hands and mouth are out of action too, so you're just gonna have to take care of yourself, buddy."

The rumble of laughter from his chest warmed me. "One day, Evie, that's all I'm giving you. Tomorrow your pussy is back in the game. We clear?"

I smacked his hands away, the hands that were doing their

best to distract me by playing with my boobs. "You're lucky I love you or else that 'we clear' bullshit you've got going on would put me out of bounds for at least another day."

He gave me another gorgeous, very distracting grin before leaving me to walk into the bathroom. "If you change your mind, I'll be in here taking care of business but you're more than fuckin' welcome to come and give me a hand," he yelled out as he moved out of sight.

I shifted onto my back and relaxed into the bed. Maybe if I closed my eyes, I could catch some more sleep while Kick did his thing in the shower. A couple of minutes later, I sat up. Who the fuck was I kidding? Knowing what he was doing only served to distract me so I got out of bed and headed into the kitchen.

I'd made us both toast and coffee by the time he joined me ten minutes later. I eyed him with a smirk. "You all good, now?"

He shook his head playfully at me and grabbed me around the waist, pulling me to him. "You do realise when I take care of business it's nowhere near as satisfying as when you do it, right? Which means I'm gonna be so frustrated by tomorrow, and *that* means I'm gonna have to bang the absolute fuck out of you to relieve my frustrations."

I laughed, and with all the innocence I could feign, I asked, "Is that one of those 'we clear' statements?"

"Fuckin' hell," he growled, his eyes flashing his need for me, "your smart mouth is going to get you into trouble one day, baby. But fuck, if I don't love it."

I kissed him and then slapped his hands away from my waist. "I made you breakfast so you have to be nice to me."

He stepped away from me and reached for his coffee. Taking a sip, he muttered, "I'm always nice to you. I'm not sure the

154

same can be said about you."

I rolled my eyes and chose to ignore his grumbling. "What are your plans for today?" I asked as I carried our plates to the table.

He followed with the coffees. "I've gotta head over to a friend's place and help him with a bike engine he's rebuilding."

"Is that one of the guys from the club?" I asked, loving the fact he was being so open.

"Yeah, Nitro. I'll probably be there most of the day. What are you up to?"

"I'm catching up with Maree. Shopping and lunch."

He leant forward in his seat and caught my lips in a kiss. "Can I have you tonight?" he asked, his eyes staring intently at me.

"You can have me every night, Kick," I said, holding his gaze, "but remember, no sex. I wasn't kidding when I said I needed a break. It's been months since I've had sex, and you're seriously wearing me out."

"Contrary to what you might think, I don't just want you for sex, sweetheart. I want a date with you tonight."

His words caused butterflies in my stomach. "I'd like that," I said softly, my heart swelling with love.

Heat continued to flash in his eyes. "Good," he said with a nod, "and baby, I never want to hear another word out of that pretty little mouth of yours about the fact you've had sex with anyone but me."

I grinned. "Okay, I can manage that," I agreed, fucking loving his jealousy. It was probably not something I *should* love and definitely something I would never encourage by flirting with another man, but it told me how much he adored me.

And I loved that.

155

"Oh my god, Maree, you're too much!"

She grinned at me and drank the remainder of her coffee. Shrugging, she said, "How am I supposed to say no when a man tells me he wants to fuck me into next week? Hell, I'm not passing this opportunity up."

She'd just filled me in on her plans for tonight and tomorrow. A guy she'd met at the gym this morning had flirted with her and talked her into a date that would obviously last them until Monday morning. I finished my coffee and agreed. "I don't blame you, I would have said hell yes, too."

"Yeah, except you have no need for first dates or one night stands anymore. Now you've got Kick to service you," she said with a wink.

I groaned. "Oh god, that man . . ."

She quirked a brow. "What's he done now? Please tell me he's got the stamina of an elite athlete."

I laughed. "He really does. My vagina is so damn sore today, like it's never been sore before."

It was her turn to groan now. "Fuck, don't tell me that. You can't tell a woman who isn't getting regular sex that your vagina has been worked into exhaustion. That shit isn't fair."

"Sorry, babe, but you asked," I said as I stood and put my sunglasses on.

She stood as well and said, "Yeah, I guess I did. I'm happy for you, Evie, you deserve happiness." I heard her genuine happiness for me in her words.

I smiled and gave her a hug. "Thank you, I'm happy for me, too."

"Okay, I've gotta go and have a pedicure and wax to get ready for my sex marathon. I'll call you on Monday and let you know if he matches your man's skills."

I laughed and watched her go. She'd done what I'd asked her to do after Jeremy's funeral – she'd given me space to work through my grief without constantly checking in with me. I loved her for it, but it was good to get out and spend time with her again.

As I turned to walk to my car, I caught a glimpse of Kick's sister. I hadn't seen Lina in over a year and I'd missed her. My heart hurt to see how much her two kids had grown. She had two little girls – Becca, the oldest, was four, and Candace, the little one, was two. It looked like they were giving their mother a hard time so I wandered over to her to see if I could give her a hand.

"Oh my goodness, Evie!" she exclaimed when she saw me, pulling me in for a hug.

My smile beamed at her. We'd grown up together and knew so much about each other. In that moment, I wished I'd never cut contact with her. "How are you, Lina?"

She frowned. "I'm actually not feeling very well, hon. I feel like I might vomit," she answered, clutching her stomach.

"Shit, are you okay to drive home or do you want me to drive you?" Looking closely at her, I could see how pale her face was. She really didn't look well at all.

"Really? You wouldn't mind driving us home?"

"Not at all," I said and took charge.

I managed to get everyone in the car and back to her place without her vomiting. Once we were through her front door, I said, "You go to bed. I'll look after the kids."

She gave me a grateful look. "Thank you," she whispered, and did as I'd said.

I turned to Becca. She was a gorgeous little red haired beauty and she gave me a smile that would melt anyone's heart. Shit, I bet she had her Uncle Kick wrapped around her finger.

157

"Are you hungry, sweetheart?" I asked as I lifted Candace up, resting her on my hip.

Becca nodded and said, "Yes. Mummy promised us cake if we were good at the shop." She stared at me expectantly and I figured I needed to either find cake or make it.

I gave her a smile and held out my hand for her. "Okay then, let's go find cake," I said as I led her towards the kitchen. Candace babbled words I could hardly discern but I figured so long as she wasn't crying we were good.

We had the batter made and ready to pour into the cake tin when loud banging came from the front of the house. I turned in that direction and my heart skipped a beat when I heard a thunderous, "Lina, open the fucking door!"

Shit, that sounded like Lina's ex, and he seemed to be in a mood. I gave my attention to Becca and with forced calmness, said, "If you take Candace into her bedroom and play with her for a little while, I'll let you have two pieces of cake when it's ready."

Her eyes widened with glee and she clapped her hands together. "Yes!" she exclaimed, and I felt relief as I watched her lead her sister out of the kitchen.

I pulled my phone out of my handbag and dialled Kick's number, willing him to answer fast.

He took what felt like ages to answer, and in that time the banging on the front door got louder. "Evie. What's up, baby?" he asked.

"Kick, can you come to Lina's house now?" I practically begged him, my voice shaking with fear.

"Fuck, what's wrong? And why are you at Lina's house?"

"Long story, and I'll fill you in later, but her ex is banging on the front door and he doesn't sound happy."

"Fuck," he swore again, "hold tight, I'll be there in about ten minutes. And whatever the fuck you do, don't let the motherfucker in."

"Okay," I promised, relieved he was on his way, but unsure I'd be able to keep Dave out because at the rate he was going, he'd have the door smashed open soon.

I shouldn't have worried, though. Kick arrived quicker than he said he would. Dave had continued to pound on the door but that was as far as he'd gotten. When I'd heard Kick's bike pull up outside, I'd finally expelled the breath I'd been holding, and rushed to Candace's room to make sure the girls were okay.

Relief surged through me at the sight of them playing quietly, unaware of what was happening out the front between their dad and their uncle. It killed me to know they'd grow up with a father like Dave. Unless he got his shit together, he was useless to them. Thank God they had their uncles.

I sat on the floor with them and asked, "Would you like me to read you a story?"

Becca gave me a huge smile and nodded emphatically. "Yes!"

I grabbed a book from the bookshelf behind me and after pulling Candace onto my lap, began reading, trying hard to block out thoughts of what Kick was taking care of. We read for about fifteen minutes until Becca looked up towards the bedroom door and squealed with delight. "Uncle Kick!" she exclaimed, and ran to him.

He caught her and scooped her up into his arms. "Hey darlin', are you being good for Evie?" he asked, his full attention on her as if she was the most important person in the world.

Oh my.

My tummy fluttered. I'd forgotten how good Kick was with kids. There was something extremely sexy to me about a man who had the time of day for the kids in his life.

I stood, taking Candace with me, and my eyes met Kick's a

159

moment later. Surprisingly, he didn't appear as if he'd just been in a fight, which I'd been expecting. I'd imagined blood smeared on his clothes or at least a much more dishevelled appearance, but he looked almost like he had when I'd left him that morning.

His concerned gaze assessed me. "You okay?" he asked softly.

I nodded. "Yes. Thank you so much for coming. Is everything sorted?"

"Yeah, he's gone, and I don't think he'll show up here like that again, but the asshole doesn't seem to learn his lessons very fast, so who knows?"

Becca smacked her uncle on the shoulder. "You said a bad word, Uncle Kick," she chastised him, a stern look written on her face.

I suppressed a laugh, and watched with interest as he handled the situation. "I'm sorry, darlin'. I'll try not to say it again, yeah?"

She pressed her lips together, trying hard to emulate her mother. I'd seen Lina give her that very look. "You're always saying bad words. I'll have to tell Mummy on you."

Laughter bubbled up, and I managed to hold it in, but I had to walk away to stop Becca from seeing my body shake with it. I took Candace into the kitchen, catching snippets of Becca telling Kick off.

When they joined us a couple of minutes later, he gave me a dirty look and said, "Thanks for that."

"For what?" I asked as I checked the cake I'd placed in the oven. The girls had scampered off to the lounge room to the television.

He grabbed me around the waist. "For leaving me alone with a four-year-old I had to defend myself to," he said, pressing a kiss to my lips.

"Well, you shouldn't use that language around her."

He groaned. "Do you know how fuckin' hard it is to stop myself from swearing around them?"

"What does Lina say?" I asked, loving seeing Kick squirm, but mostly just loving the fact he cared about it.

Lina's voice came from behind me. "Lina tells him not to do it, but do you think anyone can tell Kick what to do?"

I laughed and turned out of Kick's embrace to face her. She looked a little better. "How are you feeling?"

"A little better," she said, walking towards us. "What word did you say?" she asked Kick, giving him a dirty look.

He held up his hands in a defensive gesture. "I didn't say fuck, that's for fuckin' sure," he muttered.

She shook her head and smacked his chest. "Well, don't say it now, for goodness' sake!"

"All I said was asshole," he admitted.

Pointing a finger at him, she bossed him, "Don't say it again. I'm gonna start charging you, I think." Giving me her attention, she said, "Thank you for this afternoon. I really appreciate it."

I grimaced. "We had a visitor while you were asleep," I admitted, not wanting to have to tell her.

At her frown, Kick stepped in with an explanation. "Dave came over. He was drunk again and bashing on the front door to be let in, so Evie called me and I came and took care of him."

"Thank you," she said, her voice full of exhaustion. "How did you get him to leave?"

"Let's just say we had words." Kick's face had that closed-off look I knew well; he had no intention of telling her what those words had been.

"Did you guys get in a fight?" Lina asked, knowing her brother well.

"No, but I'm telling you, Lina, that if he keeps turning up like he did today, we *will* be having more than words."

She opened her mouth to say something but a knock at the door interrupted us.

Shit, who was it now?

"Wait here," Kick said as he strode to the front door and opened it. "Fuck," he muttered, and I wondered who the hell it was, "what are you doing here?"

A voice I hadn't heard in years sounded, and my stomach dropped. "Well, that's a lovely way to greet your mother, Kick."

Chapter Fourteen

Kick

Fuck, could this day get any worse?

I stepped aside and let my mother enter. Actually, I had no choice, because she barged her way in before I could stop her. I closed the door after her and turned to see Evie's face had paled. She looked like she'd seen a ghost, and I guessed she had.

My mother.

The reason for so much of her heartache growing up.

"Mum," Lina said, sounding anything but pleased to see her, "what are you doing here?"

Mum's back stiffened. "Am I not allowed to visit my daughter and grandchildren?"

Jesus, bring on the fucking guilt trip.

Lina scowled. "You never just drop by out of the blue. Not unless you want something." The unspoken accusation sat between them.

Mum's hand went to her hip and I could just imagine the superior look on her face. "That's not true -" She stopped mid-sentence and her head turned to look at Evie. "What the hell are *you* doing here? I thought my son had seen the error of his ways years ago." Before Evie could respond, Mum looked at me and said, "Please don't tell me she's here because you are?"

I stalked to where she stood, and, fuming, said, "You don't get to come here and say that shit to or about Evie." My body buzzed with anger at her attitude, and my breaths were coming hard and fast. "Besides, what I do is none of your business anymore."

"Yes, you made that perfectly clear two years ago, Kick, but just because you stop seeing me and try to tell me what is and what isn't my business, doesn't mean I'm not interested to know what's happening in your life." Her eyes were still as vacant as they'd been my entire life. The words were coming out of her mouth but she didn't mean them.

My mother. The shallowest woman I'd ever had the misfortune of knowing.

"You've never been interested in my life," I spat. "The only thing Veronica Hanson is interested in is Veronica Hanson."

Her eyes flared with anger. And a tiny bit of hatred. My mother held a lot of resentment in her soul, and her kids and husband had been wrapped up in that resentment for years. We'd held her back; stifled her life plans. Apparently. "How the hell did you come from me?" she demanded to know.

"That's a really good fuckin' question."

"Kick!" Lina interjected, her eyes glaring at me.

Fuck, the fuckin' swearwords.

I quickly glanced at the kids who were busy watching television. Thank fuck, they didn't need to be involved in this shit. I turned back to my mother. "I don't know how the hell any of your kids turned out okay after being subjected to your nastiness and bitchiness while we were growing up, but you did manage to screw Evie up, so there *is* that."

Evie caught my attention when she took a step in my direction, a distraught look on her face. She found my eyes and whatever she saw there stopped her. "Kick . . ." she began, but I cut her off.

"No, Evie, she needs to hear this. So her husband screwed around on her and then took it one step further and slept with

164

her best friend. It doesn't give her the right to take that shit out on the kids in her life, one of them being you. Just because her husband slept with your mother doesn't give her the fuckin' right to label *you* . . . a fuckin' innocent teenager in all that . . . a slut, and spread nasty rumours about you." My heart pumped furiously in my chest as years of hurt and anger roared to the surface. I jabbed my finger at my mother. "*That shit ain't fuckin' right!*"

Jesus!

I began pacing in the small space I occupied, fully aware I was close to losing my shit completely. Evie and Lina stared at me in horror. None of this had ever been confronted. Our families had splintered apart after Evie's sister died, and we'd shattered completely after Dad slept with Loretta six months later. As far as I was concerned, this conversation was about eighteen years too late.

"You've got no idea what I went through! What your father did to me!" my mother screamed at me, the vacant look in her eyes long gone, replaced with bitterness and pure hatred.

"I don't give a *shit* what my father did to you! You should have been more concerned about your children but instead, *I* spent my whole life chasing your affection . . . chasing your love. *You* were more concerned with trying to make yourself look good so that people would think you were this amazing mother and amazing person when that was so damn far from the truth."

She stared wildly at me, her chest heaving, and her face flushed with anger. "You've grown into an asshole, Kick. That club is obviously no good for you but that's what you get for abandoning your family as soon as you could."

Was she for fucking real?

Funny how someone's memories of how something went

165

down can be so wrong.

I jabbed my finger at her again, the adrenaline coursing through my veins needing an outlet, and a finger jab seemed like a much better option than the punch I wanted to throw. I'd never punch a woman, but the wall was looking more and more attractive. The kids were the only things holding me back at this point. "I joined Storm because they were more of a family to me than you and Dad ever were," I fumed. "You can't abandon something that isn't there in the first place. Dad was long gone, and you were never there. And I never fuckin' abandoned Lina or Braden."

The rage circling the room threatened to choke me.

I need to get out of here.

Without another glance at my mother, I turned and stalked out of the house. Once I'd made it to the footpath, I placed my hands behind my head to grip the back of my neck. "Fuck!" I roared into the air, pushing a chunk of pent up frustration out.

I paced the footpath for a few minutes until Mum came storming out of the house towards her car. "Don't ever talk to me again, Kick. I don't want anything to do with you ever again!" she yelled as she threw her bag in the car.

"Consider it done!" I thundered, and turned my back as she backed out of the driveway and sped off. "Fuck!" I yelled again, desperately trying to get the rage out that was trapped in my body.

Evie came running out of the house, towards me. I held my hand up, signalling for her to stop, to not come anywhere near me, because I couldn't be sure of my actions at the moment.

She slowed her advance but didn't stop, her eyes pleading with me to let her close.

To let her in.

"No, Evie, don't come any closer!" I yelled, hating the words as they left my lips but unable to stop them from falling out. I needed to keep her safe and *I* wasn't safe.

She didn't fucking stop.

She came right up to me and a moment later, her hand landed on my arm. "Kick," she said, her voice calm.

Full of love.

My mind flickered with a chaotic mess of thoughts.

So jumbled.

So confused.

I tried to claw through them but instead I was drowning in them.

I was drowning in my life.

A childhood of abandonment, an adolescence of hurt and grief, a life of regret.

Her arms circled me. "Kick," she soothed me as she pulled me close.

Love.

Evie's love clawed through the thoughts.

It pushed the pain aside as it reached for my heart.

For my soul.

Home.

Family.

Evie is my family.

I took a deep breath and put my arms around her. "Evie," I whispered, "I love you."

Her hand ran up and down my neck, in and out of my hair. "I love you, too, baby," she whispered.

I clung to her for a long time, allowing the anger and hurt to seep out of me. Eventually, I pulled away from Evie and asked, "How did you know?"

She frowned. "How did I know what?"

"That I needed you. That it would be okay to ignore me and

come to me even when I told you not to," I said, not letting her eyes go, needing them to stay with me and silently tell me the secrets of her heart that her words couldn't.

And they did. The love shone from them as she said, "I knew, because I know you would never hurt me, Kick. You've *always* made sure I was okay, made sure no one else was hurting me. I know deep in my bones that there will *never* come a day that you hurt me."

I gently placed my hand against her cheek. "You never gave up on me, did you?" I whispered.

She shook her head. "No."

I bent my face and kissed her.

Deep and searching.

I'd had her words and I'd had her eyes. Now I needed her body to tell me how much she loved me. When her hands slid over my back and her lips blessed mine with a kiss that reached right into my soul, I knew she was completely in.

I knew Evie would love me forever.

Just like I'd loved her forever.

Chapter Fifteen

Evie

"Shit," I muttered as I turned the mower off and collapsed onto the newly mowed grass. I ran my forearm across my sweaty forehead, trying to stop the drops of sweat falling into my eyes.

Why did I have the bright idea to mow this afternoon?

On one of the hottest days of the year so far.

At least it had taken my mind off the huge blow-up between Kick and his mother a couple of days ago. I'd never seen him lose it like that at his family before, but he'd definitely needed to get it out because I'd noticed a change in him since. He didn't seem as angry or hard as he had been for years.

I couldn't deny I'd loved how he defended me, too. Veronica had been awful to me after my mother slept with her husband, and a lot of my problems in my last two years of school had been as a direct result of her vindictiveness. Kick had clearly recognised that and held onto his anger over it for all these years.

I sighed and lay back on the grass. Closing my eyes, I thought about where he and I were at now. We were together in a way we'd never been together. He'd opened himself up to me completely, and I felt safe in the haven our relationship had become.

A low whistle sounded from behind me, and I opened my eyes and sat up to find Kick walking towards me with a grin on his face. My body thrummed with desire. This man just had to catch my attention and I was gone. When he stepped into my view looking the way he did this afternoon, I knew it would be hard not to jump him and demand sex. Between the muscles his jeans and white t-shirt barely contained, his confident swagger, and the ruggedly handsome face I'd memorised deep in my heart, I didn't have a hope in hell of not throwing myself at him. Oh, and add to all of that the beard he'd grown, and I was going down.

Happily.

"Why are you mowing?" he asked as he sat next to me, stretching his legs out in front of him and his arms out behind him, leaning back on his hands.

"Because, funnily enough, the grass grew," I answered him with the smart mouth I knew he loved.

"Smartass," he muttered, the grin not leaving his face. "Leave it for me in the future, okay?"

I raised my brows. "Is that an 'okay' type statement or a 'we clear' type statement?" I couldn't resist, and waited to see what he'd do next. My body kinda hoped he'd attack it.

He didn't disappoint, and a moment later, I was lying back on the grass with Kick on top of me. Bending his face close to mine, he growled, "It's a 'we clear' statement, baby, but perhaps you need to be reminded who wears the pants in this relationship."

Oh god, yes, I do.

I bit my lip and stared at him, willing him to keep going.

To show me who wore the pants.

His eyes searched mine, questioning. "Yeah?" he asked.

I decided to push him, just to make sure he pursued this. "I think we know who wears the pants when all is said and done," I said in my sweetest voice. "You might think it's you, but it's

170

not."

Heat flashed in those beautiful green eyes of his and he reared up, ripping his shirt off. Next his hands went to my shorts, which he stripped off, along with my panties. He bent his face back to mine and claimed my lips in a rough kiss before saying, "I'm not seeing any pants on you, baby."

Sitting back up to straddle me, he undid his jeans and pulled his cock out. He wrapped his hand around it and stroked it a couple of times, his gaze never leaving mine, except to take in my tongue licking my lips.

The fact we were in my backyard turned me on so damn much. And I knew it would be turning Kick on, too. He liked to fuck out in the open, and we'd had sex in a lot of strange places over the years.

"Babe, you with me?" he asked, snapping my attention back to what he was doing.

"Yeah, I'm waiting patiently for you to show me who the man is," I said, goading him.

"Darlin', this is about so much more than showing you who the man is, 'cause I think we can both agree who the fuckin' man is here." His lips brushed over mine again, his teeth lightly biting them. With his gaze firmly fixed to mine, he reached a hand down to my pussy and pushed two fingers in. Rough and hard, causing my body to slide a little. "*No*, this is about showing you who owns your body." He slid his fingers out and then pushed them both back in, hard again, and I moaned at the pleasure he caused.

He kept this up, working me towards heaven.

Working me towards admitting to him who owned my body. Although, it wasn't really a secret.

He'd almost brought me to orgasm when he pulled his fingers out and moved his hands to my t-shirt. Pushing it up to expose my breasts, he then pulled my bra cups down to let my breasts fall out and into his mouth.

My pussy cried out her need, and I begged, "Kick, what the fuck?"

He had a handful and mouthful of boob and wasn't letting go, but his eyes looked up at mine in a 'what?' glance.

"You had me so close, baby,' I complained.

He let my boob fall out of his mouth. "Really?" he asked with a smug look on his face.

Fine. If that was how he wanted to play this, two could play at that game. "It's all good, I can take care of this," I said as I reached down to bring myself to orgasm.

He sat back and watched as I pushed my fingers inside and did what I really wanted him to do. I thought for sure he would take over, but he didn't. Instead, he took hold of his dick and began pumping it while keeping his eyes trained on my pussy.

Fuck.

My plan had backfired, but I had another one up my sleeve.

I quickly sat up and moved so I could push him onto his back and straddle him. Positioning myself over his cock, I pushed down to take him inside.

"Fuck!" he roared as his face clearly showed the pleasure I was giving him.

His hands came to my hips and held me tight as I fucked him.

He'd already worked me up with his fingers so I wasn't far off, and the angle I was fucking him at now always got me there faster. As I felt my orgasm about to explode around me, I fucked him harder and faster, desperate for it.

We came together and both cried out our pleasure. I pressed my hands against his chest as I took every last drop of heaven I could find. When I finally opened my eyes, I found him watching me with lust-filled eyes.

I moved off him so I could lay on the grass next to him, curled into his side, head on his arm that had come around my shoulders. "I guess I wear the pants in this relationship," I murmured against his chest.

His body gently shook as he chuckled. "Was there any fuckin' doubt, sweetheart?"

I smiled and closed my eyes.

I loved my man, but I *really* loved how he let me think I had some control when we both knew neither of us had any control.

Our hearts ruled us.

And we each ruled each other.

***

The next morning, Kick made me run late for a dentist appointment after fucking me in bed and then again in the shower. I was running around my house like a mad woman trying to get everything together when the dentist's receptionist called to move my appointment to a later time slot. I rescheduled with her and then dropped my phone into my bag, relieved I now had a chance to calm down and get ready without the panic.

Kick grinned and came towards me, his hands reaching for the button on my jeans. I slapped his hand away. "No," I said firmly, giving him the evil eye. "You've had your fill this morning and I'm all out of orgasms."

He smirked. "Baby, you are *never* out of orgasms."

I raised my brows, trying to look stern. "I am today."

Crossing his arms over his chest, he said, "So you've got a dentist appointment and then what?"

"Then I've got work. Why?"

"I'm just trying to figure out how long until I can get my dick

173

out again." When I smirked, he added, "You don't seem to realise just what you do to me, Evie."

I put my hand on my hip, settling in to hear this. "Tell me, Kick, what do I do to you?"

He uncrossed his arms and took the few strides separating us. "You cause an insatiable fuckin' need in me that I've never experienced before. Even if I fucked you all day long, I'd still never get enough."

Oh god.

My core clenched.

Maybe I *did* have more orgasms in me today.

He traced my lips and then cupped my cheek before kissing me. "I'm taking you to your appointment and then to work, and then I'm picking you up from work and taking you back to my house. Today we play my way. With my toys," he growled, and I felt his growl all the way through my body.

Hell yes.

He slapped my ass and said, "Hurry up and finish getting ready. We need to make a quick detour past my place on the way."

I did as I was told, and fifteen minutes later he had me on the back of his bike and we were on our way to his house. As I hugged him, I couldn't stop thinking about how good it was to have him back in my life. Thank goodness for second chances, and even third chances. I knew some people hated the idea of love the second time around because they felt it meant so much wasted time, and while I agreed, I truly believed that sometimes you just weren't ready for each other the first time. Or in mine and Kick's case, the second time.

We dropped by Kick's place and he picked something up before we headed to my dentist. I was surprised when he made another detour on the way. We pulled up outside a rundown house and I wondered who lived here. I hopped off his bike and removed my helmet, waiting for him to tell me what we were doing here. However, he simply took his helmet off, dumped it on his bike, grabbed my hand and led me towards the front door.

After he knocked, I asked, "What are we doing here, Kick?"

He seemed so serious. "You'll see."

A guy dressed in what looked to be thrift shop clothing opened the door and ushered us in. He also seemed very serious, and I felt a little anxious, but at the same time, I knew Kick wouldn't put me in harm's way so this must be a safe place.

"Thanks for coming, man. She wasn't supposed to be here until tomorrow, but her old man beat her up bad enough last night for her to leave earlier, and I just want to get her out of town as soon as possible," the guy said to Kick.

"No worries, Brian, I'm just fuckin' glad she's finally decided enough's enough. And King will be, too."

Brian eyed me over his shoulder and then looked at Kick. "This your woman?"

"Yeah, eyes off," Kick replied firmly, his message loud and clear.

Brian held his hands up. "Hey, no problem, I've got enough to worry about with my old lady. I got no clue how men handle more than one woman at a time."

Kick chuckled, but all traces of humour were gone when we made it into a bedroom at the back of the house. Sitting on a bed was a woman who looked to be just under thirty. I sucked in a breath at the sight of her face. Her old man had done some serious damage; she could hardly see out of one eye and the rest of her face was heavily bruised, as was her neck and upper chest area. I shuddered to think what her clothes hid.

Kick knelt in front of her, his face a mask of anger. "Fuck,

Jen . . ." His voice trailed off as he took in her bruises.

She winced as she tried to speak. "I'm here now, yeah?"

He nodded and swore under his breath again. "We're getting you out of Sydney today, and I don't want to ever see you back here again."

She agreed, and Kick stood. He walked out of the room, and after Brian spoke to the woman for a couple of minutes, he followed Kick out.

"You've told King she's here?" Kick asked as he pulled an envelope out of his jacket pocket and handed it to Brian.

"Yeah, he's going to swing by a little later today to see her before she leaves," Brian answered, opening the envelope and flicking through the wads of cash inside.

I was stunned. There had to be thousands in that envelope.

Kick frowned. "It's all there, as promised," he muttered.

Brian shoved the envelope in his pocket. "Thanks, I appreciate it."

"I'll let you know when I have more," Kick promised, and then grabbed my hand and led me out of the house.

I was glad to walk outside. Not only was that house rundown, it felt depressing inside, with old furniture and little decoration. Kick seemed on a mission to get back to his bike, but I tugged on his hand to slow him down. When he looked back at me with a questioning glance, I asked, "What was that about?"

He stopped walking and turned to face me. Jerking his chin towards the house, he said, "That's a safe house for battered women, and we help them escape their motherfucker husbands and boyfriends and get them out of Sydney."

"Who's 'we'?"

"King, Brian and me."

"And where did you get all that money from?" I asked the

176

question I figured he might not answer, but there was no harm in trying.

He sucked in a breath and avoided my eyes for a moment, but he surprised me when he looked back at me and said, "I got it off a druggie scum-of-the-earth asshole, and trust me babe, you don't want to know what happened to him, but let's just say the earth breathed a little easier that day." He finished talking and then waited for my reply, his eyes wary. He had no need to worry, though, because I had no problems with the earth breathing a little easier.

I gave him a smile that I hoped told him how I felt. "So you were just redistributing the wealth, so to speak?"

He stared at me for just a moment longer with that serious gaze, and then broke out in a smile. I watched as his shoulders loosened and his breathing evened out. "Yeah, you could say that. King leaves me in charge of financing the operation so whenever we come across extra cash, I put it aside." He paused for a moment before giving me a regretful look. "I wish I could have given you that money to bail your Dad out, but it was already promised to Brian by then."

"You don't have to explain yourself, Kick. And besides, you found another way to help."

He nodded, but didn't say anything.

"Who was that woman?" I asked quietly. I had the sense she was more than just a stranger who needed help.

"Jen is an ex of King's. They dated a long time ago, and she left him for the asshole who nearly ended up killing her."

I had never met King before, but he sounded like a good guy if he still looked out for an ex, as well as all these other women who needed help. "I'd like to meet King one day," I said softly.

He smiled again. "I can organise that, baby," he said, giving me something I had wanted for a very long time.

He'd given me a piece of himself he'd kept hidden for so long by promising to introduce me to his friend.

"Thank you," I whispered, feeling like we'd just taken another huge step towards our future.

***

"What are you doing home alone? I thought you and Kick couldn't get enough of each other these days," Maree said into the phone.

I tucked the phone between my ear and my shoulder to free my hands. "We were going to spend the afternoon playing with his toys but he had to do some club work," I said as I grabbed the ice cream out of the fridge.

"Fuck, you're a lucky woman. What kind of toys are we talking here? And shit, it's nine pm babe, why isn't he back yet?"

I laughed, scooping ice cream into my mouth. "I think he meant his remote control car, shit like that," I joked with her.

I could picture her poking her tongue at me. "Very funny, Evie."

"Well, seriously, what kind of toys do you think he meant? Mind you, I think Kick could even make playing with a remote control car sexy."

She sighed. "I think you're probably right."

"We'll have to play another day, though. He rang about half an hour ago and said he'd be busy for a while so he'd see me tomorrow."

"Bugger. You'll have to play with BOB instead."

She spoke the truth. I'd been horny all day imagining amazing sex with Kick, so I'd have to take care of that myself now. "I should video it and send it to him."

She started coughing and spluttering. "God, you just made me almost choke on my drink. I think that'd be an awesome idea. Serves him right for cancelling on you."

I put the lid back on the ice cream and placed the tub back in the freezer. Taking hold of my phone again, I began walking to my bedroom. "I was kidding, Maree. Whatever he's doing obviously needs his attention and if I sent him that, he'd be so distracted."

"I guess," she mused, not sounding convinced, "but I'd still send it."

"That's cause you're a bitch and like your men to pay when they don't make good on promises."

Laughing, she agreed, "Yeah, I do."

A noise outside distracted me and caused my heart rate to spike.

Shit, was that someone out there?

"Maree, I think there's someone outside my house. Can you stay on the phone while I go and check?"

"Fuck . . . yeah, go," she said, her voice tinged with concern.

"Thanks," I said as I switched the outside lights on and slid the back door open. I took a tentative step, not seeing or hearing anyone, but that noise had pretty much convinced me someone had been out here.

My back door opened up onto a cemented outside entertainment area that then led to a brick path that took me down the side of my house to the front. I found one of my pot plants had been knocked over, the dirt spilling onto the cement.

Shit.

My breathing picked up and my heart thumped in my chest.

"Can you see anyone?" Maree whispered into the phone.

"No, but someone's been here because the pot plant is knocked over," I whispered back, not really sure why the fuck I was whispering when this was my house.

And then I heard my side gate latch, and my heart fell into my stomach.

I wasn't sure whether to move towards the sound or away from it, but my instincts took over and my legs began walking towards the gate. I switched my phone's flashlight on and shone it down the side of the house, expecting to come face to face with the intruder any second.

I saw nothing. The gate was shut and the path was clear. I hurried through the gate to the front yard, just in time to hear a squeal of tires and a car speeding off down the street. The car was so far away I couldn't even work out the make or model.

I switched off the flashlight and put the phone back to my ear to hear Maree screeching at me.

"Shhh," I said, "he's gone, and I'm okay."

"Oh my god, don't ever do that to me again, Evie! I was asking you if you were okay and you weren't answering me! Do you have any idea how many grey hairs you just gave me?"

"Sorry, but I needed the flashlight to see."

"Fuck, so there *was* someone there?"

I tried to calm down from the fright and get my breathing under control. "Yes, there was definitely someone here." I'd made it back inside and locked the door behind me, but I was leaving the outside lights on tonight. It probably wouldn't stop someone intent on getting in, but I felt better having them on.

"Christ, you need to call Kick and get him over to stay with you tonight."

"No, I don't want to bug him. And besides, there have been a few break-ins around here lately so it was probably someone trying to get in, and now I've scared him off. I doubt he'll be back. I'll call the police in the morning," I said, feeling too exhausted to wait for them to come out tonight. And besides, what could they do anyway? It wasn't like the cops had the resources to position someone on our street just waiting for a burglar to come by.

"Do you want me to come and stay?" she asked, being the wonderful friend she was.

"No, I'm okay," I said, "but thanks, babe."

"Mmmm . . . I'm not convinced I shouldn't come over."

"Maree, I have security on the house. I'm locked up tight and no fucker is getting in tonight. I promise, I'm all good."

She was silent for a few moments and then conceded. "Okay, but you call me the minute you are worried. And I'll be calling you in the morning to check on you."

We ended the call, and I crawled into bed.

It was probably a good thing Kick wasn't here. He'd go all crazy protective, and while I loved his bossy way in the bedroom, I didn't need him trying to control my every movement.

Chapter Sixteen

Kick

I pocketed the cash we'd just collected for King, and turned to Nitro as we headed towards our bikes. "I like it when jobs are that easy."

He nodded. "Yeah, makes it a lot fucking easier when they just pay up with no encouragement needed."

Just as we reached our bikes, my phone rang. King. "What's up, brother?" I answered it.

"Have you been to Hawk's to collect yet?"

"Nope."

"Good, cancel that job. I'm gonna give him an extra week to pay," he said, stunning me. King rarely gave extensions.

"Yeah, the motherfucker's mother needed cash for an operation so I figure she needs it more than us."

"You believe him?"

"He wasn't the one who told me. Jen told me when I saw her yesterday before she left."

I was so confused, not understanding the connection between Jen and Hawk, but I figured King knew his shit. "Right, so we're done for the day then. I'll bring the cash back now, but do you need me after that?" I hadn't seen Evie since yesterday afternoon and was fucking craving her.

"No, you and Nitro can call it a day."

"Thanks. I'll see you soon with this cash," I promised before ending the call.

Nitro raised his brows. "We done for the day?"

I nodded. "Yeah, man." I reached for my helmet. "Did you finish working on the engine?"

"It's nearly done. Thanks for your help the other day."

"Sure. Just call out if you need a hand again."

My phone buzzed with another call, and my face broke out in a grin when I saw the caller ID.

Evie.

Nitro chuckled. "Looks like some good pussy there, brother."

"Yeah, you could say that," I said as I answered it. "What's up, baby?" I said into the phone.

"Someone's broken into my house . . . can you come over? It's okay if you can't, but -"

I was instantly on alert; Evie sounded panicked. "I'll be there in about ten minutes. Are you okay until then?"

"Yes. Thank you," she said softly, relief clear in her voice.

"Fuck," I muttered as I shoved my phone in my pocket.

"What's up?" Nitro asked.

"My girlfriend's house has been broken into."

"You need help?"

"Nah, should be alright," I said, turning over the engine of my bike.

He nodded, and I gave him a chin lift. "I'll catch you later, man." And then I took off for Evie's place.

Whoever had broken into her house would pay dearly.

***

I'd expected to find Evie still panicked, but she'd calmed down by the time I got there. I took in the mess as I walked through the house to find her in the kitchen. The place had been

183

trashed and it looked like we had a big clean up ahead of us.

She looked up from the table where she sat. "Thank God you're here," she said as she got up and came to me.

I opened my arms and pulled her close. She gratefully stepped into my embrace and rested her head against my chest. I felt the tightness of her body, and rubbed my hand up and down her back. I held her until she lifted her head and looked up into my eyes.

"Why did they have to wreck the place as well?" she asked, her voice cracking a little.

"Fuck . . ." I swore, "because they're assholes."

"Yeah, they are." She let me go and walked to the sink. "I need a coffee. You want one?"

"No, I'm gonna take a look around." At her nod, I headed into the lounge room and surveyed the damage. It didn't look like anything of real value had been taken. The television and stereo were still here. I walked around the entire house and then back into the kitchen. "Babe, what's actually missing?" I asked, because I couldn't work out what had been taken. All big-ticket items seemed to be in place.

She was on the phone, on hold, and she answered, "That's the weird thing. I can't work out what's been stolen."

"Who are you on the phone to?"

"The cops."

I reached for the phone and she let me take it. Ending the call, I said, "I don't think anything's missing, unless they took jewellery or something smaller like that?"

"No, I checked that, and nothing is missing."

"Do you want to claim this on insurance?"

She frowned. "I don't know. Why?"

"If you want to claim it you'll have to involve the cops. If not, you can forget them and just let me and the boys find out

184

who did it, and deal with them for you. Either way I'll be finding out who did it, but I'd prefer not to have the cops involved."

She thought about it for a moment and then said, "I'll just let you handle it."

I gave her a quick kiss and said, "Okay, I'm gonna get started on it now. Will you be alright on your own?"

She gave me a smile and nodded. "Yeah, Maree said she'd come over if I need her, so I'll give her a call. She'll help me clean up, too."

Thank fuck for her friend. I didn't really want to leave her on her own.

As I headed out, I mulled it over. My natural instinct would be to suspect Gambarro because I was a paranoid bastard, but this didn't seem like a job he would pull.

It seemed to me that if he were involved, Evie wouldn't be breathing anymore.

But it wouldn't hurt to check in on him.

***

"Mr Gambarro is out of the country." His security guy glared down at me, challenging me to argue with him. He was refusing me entry to Gambarro's building and feeding me stories about Gambarro not being here.

"You expect me to buy that?"

"I don't give a fuck if you do or don't; it's the truth. Now fuck off and leave me alone."

I assessed the situation and decided to confirm that information with my other contacts before pursuing this any further, but I did ask, "When will he be back?"

The guy glared at me harder, in a 'you're-fucking-kidding-me' look. "I said, fuck off."

I pulled out my phone and began dialling as I walked away.

Bones answered on almost the first ring. "Kick. What's up, my man?"

I liked Bones, simply because he usually had solid information, and he was always willing to share it with me. He ran strip clubs and girls, and, in general, had his finger in a lot of pies. "Do you know if Gambarro is out of the country?"

"Yeah, he left last week. Pretty sure he'll be back this week, maybe in a couple of days."

"Thanks for that."

"Why do you ask?" Bones was a nosy motherfucker and while he had his uses, I didn't trust him with my secrets.

"Just checking some shit out for a friend. Their place was trashed, and they suspect him, but I don't figure him for that kind of thing."

"Yeah, it doesn't sound like something he would pull. Gambarro would be in your face; you'd know it was him without a shadow of a doubt."

"My thoughts exactly. Thanks, man, I'll keep investigating and figure out who else it could be," I said and then ended the call.

No doubt that information would start spreading and perhaps whoever was responsible would come to light sooner rather than later.

***

I headed to the clubhouse after that and found King in the bar. *The newly painted bar.* He was on one of the old couches with one of the club whores. Brittany had gotten her way with the new paint but not with the new couches. There'd been no point really; new couches would only get used in the same way the old ones did.

King dragged his attention away from the ass he'd been admiring to look at me. "You come to play, Kick?" he asked with a wicked glint in his eye.

"No, I've got your money for you, plus I need to talk to you about something."

He slapped the whore's ass and moved her so he could stand. "Wait here, I won't be long," he ordered her before leading me to the office.

I shut the office door behind me and handed him the envelope of cash. "My girlfriend's house was broken into today. They trashed it, but I don't think they stole anything."

He punched in the code to the safe and dumped the cash in it. Turning back to me, he asked, "Are you thinking this is retaliation from Gambarro? Or Silver Hell?"

"Fuck, I hadn't thought of Silver Hell, but I *had* considered Gambarro for it. Doesn't seem to fit his usual style, though."

Shaking his head, he said, "No, it doesn't." He sat in the chair behind the desk, a thoughtful look on his face. I waited for him to speak. "What about Silver Hell, though? Did you find out anything else about where they are at with Marco's death?"

"Last I heard they were chasing up a lead that Black Deeds were involved in that. They weren't even looking in our direction so I don't think this is their work, either. It's too subtle."

He shrugged. "Maybe you and I are just too fucking paranoid for our own good, brother. Maybe this is your run-of-the-mill neighbourhood burglary and has nothing to do with us."

"Yeah, could be. I'll keep looking into it."

King's eyes narrowed on me. "This chick means something to you?"

"Evie means everything to me," I stated, aware this would trigger further questions from him.

"As much as the club means to you?"

"My loyalties are even."

He was silent for a moment, and then he blew out a long breath. "Well, fuck, I never thought I'd see the day," he murmured.

"Is that a problem for you?" I really fucking hoped it wouldn't be because it might force me to admit to myself, and everyone else, that my loyalties actually weren't even. That my loyalties were fast becoming slanted more in Evie's direction.

Standing, he said, "No, brother. She means something to you, then she means something to the club. We're behind you with this. Whatever you need, you've got." His eyes bore into mine and told me he meant every word he said.

I let out the breath I didn't realise I'd been holding. Nodding, I said, "Thanks."

Contemplating that conversation as I headed back to Evie's house, I realised how deep I was in with Evie. Seventeen years of club loyalty meant more to me than anything else in my life. But not more than Evie meant to me.

And fuck, I didn't know what to make of that.

Chapter Seventeen

Evie

Kick arrived back at my house about two hours after he'd left. Maree and I had cleaned up most of the mess the intruders had made, and we were now in the kitchen discussing the break-ins that had been occurring in the neighbourhood lately. Kick entered the kitchen and the energy shifted immediately. He stopped and stared at me, a look of pure need in his eyes. But there was something else there, something I couldn't quite put my finger on straight away.

Maree sensed it, too, and gave me a look that said *'fuck, I am getting out of here so you can get laid'*. She grabbed her bag and said, "I'll call you tomorrow and make sure you're okay."

"Thanks for your help, babe," I said as she left.

Kick didn't take his eyes off me. As soon as the front door closed behind Maree, he came to me. His hand went straight to the button on my shorts and a moment later it was in my panties, searching for my slit. No words were exchanged; our eyes did all the talking. And Kick's eyes were loud. And dark. If I didn't know him as well as I did, I would be scared of his intentions.

His finger roughly entered me, and he hissed. Pushing in deep, he began fucking me with it. My eyes rolled shut, and he growled, "Keep your eyes open, Evie. I want to watch them as you come."

I shuddered at the hardness in his voice and in his eyes. This was the Hard Kick, and I didn't know him so well. I realised I had no idea where this would go tonight. So I did as he said. Kick was completely in charge of tonight.

While his fingers fucked me, his other hand came to my cheek, and he roughly grasped me, his thumb tracing my lips. Our eyes remained locked and our breathing matched in its shallowness.

Oh god, I was going to come.

I was going to come hard.

"Let it go, baby," he commanded, knowing my body so well. Knowing I was so close. "But keep your eyes open."

The rough authority in his voice did it in the end. I came, forcing my eyes to stay open the entire time. My whole body exploded with pleasure, and my legs threatened to give way under me. Kick's arms came around me, and he lifted me and carried me into my bedroom.

A moment later I was on my feet and he'd quickly stripped me. I stood naked in front of him, his eyes hungrily running over my body. He'd already brought me to orgasm once, but I could feel it building again, simply from the intense hunger radiating from him.

I needed to touch him, but when I took a step in his direction, he barked, "No." His eyes snapped back to mine, and he lifted his tee over his head, and then removed the rest of his clothes. His cock was rock hard, and my pussy screamed for it, but I did as he said and stood still, waiting for his next move.

Desire slid right through me when he reached for the handcuffs sitting on my bedside table. "I want you on your back on the bed, with your arms above your head," he ordered, his voice hard, not containing one scrap of the gentle, fun Kick.

And I fucking loved the shiver it gave me, from the unpredictability of him.

I did as he said and waited.

He remained standing, his eyes on mine. I couldn't be sure, but it seemed he was weighing something up in his mind. It seemed like he was at war with his need.

"Kick -" I began, but he cut me off.

"Don't talk," he bossed me, his breaths starting to come hard and fast. And then he muttered, "Fuck." He shoved his hand through his hair, and turned around and walked out of the room.

What the hell?

I shifted so I could lean on my elbows and see where he went, but he'd moved out of my line of sight. Moving off the bed, I went in search of him, finding him in the lounge room, his back to me, his shoulders tense.

"What's wrong, Kick?" I asked quietly, almost afraid of the answer. I'd always wanted to know this side of Kick, but his intensity was freaking me out a little.

He turned to me, his eyes flashing anger, and that scared me even more. I hadn't done anything to earn that anger. When he finally spoke, his voice was strangled, broken almost. "I'm mad at you . . . and I don't want to be mad at you . . ."

I frowned, unable to understand the words coming out of his mouth. "I don't understand," I almost whispered.

"Fuck! Neither do I," he said, agitated.

I stayed silent.

Waiting for him to explain further.

Hoping this wasn't the end of us.

His gaze roared with fury and violence.

And I didn't understand.

My heart cracked a little more, the scars of our love aching. It seemed that's all we were destined for. Scars and hurt. And an inability to make this work.

"I love you, Evie," he started and then stopped abruptly, like

191

he was searching for the right words. "But I fuckin' hate the power you have over me." His words bled with the conflict he was obviously experiencing. "Fuck, that didn't come out right," he muttered. His eyes pleaded with me to understand, begged me not to walk away from this, but rather to stay and fight.

And so that's what I did.

I fought for Kick.

I moved to him, and placed my hand on his chest. He flinched, but I ignored it. Kick needed my love. He needed to know this would be okay, and that we would battle our way through any obstacles that came at us. My counsellor instincts kicked in. "What power do I have over you?"

He took a deep breath and I felt his heart beating fast in his chest. "You have the power to fuck my loyalties up." His words were raw and honest, and I loved him even more for that. I loved that he gave me that because it meant we could go forward from a place of truth.

"Your loyalty to your club?"

"Yes." His voice was forceful, demanding, as if he wanted me to fix it for him.

But I couldn't fix this for him. I could only try to help him sort through the mess of emotions and thoughts rushing at him.

"Why does your love for me have to affect that, Kick? Why can't you have loyalty to both of us?"

"Because if shit ever goes down, it could mean that one day I will have to make a choice. You or the club."

Clarity hit me square in the chest. "That's the real reason why you kept walking away from me, isn't it?' I asked quietly.

He stared at me for a long time, processing that. And then his face contorted in torment and he nodded. "I think so," he whispered, "but I never realised that until just now."

I asked the one question that had to be answered in order for us to take another step on this journey together. The answer to this question would determine our future. "Can you get past that anger at me?" I held my breath, waiting for him to reply.

Willing him to say the one word I desperately wanted him to say.

"I'm not angry at you, baby. I'm angry at myself." His gaze softened, and my heart soared at his admission, but it confused me even further.

My eyebrows drew together. "Why?"

The air crackled with his ferocious love. It blazed for me to see and feel. "Because I love you, and I've always fuckin' loved you. I might not like the power you have over me, but I'm fuckin' angry with myself for even thinking I should put you second to the club. You've always come first, and you always will. I just couldn't admit that to myself until today."

We'd had many moments of honesty since we'd found each other again, but I felt this one deep in my heart. This really was a defining moment for us and I needed to find a way to show Kick that I got it, that I understood the depth of his feelings for me.

I moved my hand from his chest to his face, gently placing it on his cheek. Shifting closer to him, I kissed his lips. His arms circled me, pulling me even closer. My arms moved up and around his neck, and my fingers worked their way into his hair. Our kiss deepened, and we expressed our love in the best way we knew how. Our lips, tongues and bodies communicated on a deeper level than our words would ever be able to.

When I ended the kiss, I said, "I want to spend the rest of my life with you, Kick. I want you to love me, and hate me, and fight with me, and make up with me, and do it over and over. I want you forever."

His arms tightened around me. "Thank fuck, 'cause you're

193

stuck with me. You're mine now, baby, and I'm yours, and there's nothing that will stop me from fighting for us."

He spent the rest of the night blessing my body with his love, and I thanked the universe for giving him back to me.

By the time my eyes closed from sheer exhaustion hours later, I knew we'd finally come full circle. The promises we'd made each other as teenagers would be fulfilled.

We'd never give up on each other again.

***

The next morning, I rushed into the kitchen to grab breakfast before heading out to work. Kick had monopolised my time again this morning, causing me to be late *again*.

He watched me from the table where he drank his coffee, and gave me a cheeky grin. God, I loved that grin, but fuck, I couldn't afford to be distracted by him again. "You okay, baby?" he asked, knowing full well I was stressing about running late.

I held my hand up at him. "Don't talk to me," I muttered as I rummaged through my bag looking for my phone. I ignored his snicker. When I couldn't locate my phone, I looked up at him, and asked, "Have you seen my phone?"

He raised his brows. "Oh, am I allowed to talk to you now?"

I put my hand on my hip and glared at him. "Very funny, smartass."

Chuckling, he stood and came to me. As he moved to pass me, he bent his face and whispered in my ear, "Look on your bedside table, sweetheart, I'm pretty sure that's where you left it." And then he kept moving to the sink to rinse his mug. And I was left with desire running through me.

Shit.

I ignored my body and its needs and hurried into the

bedroom to grab my phone. He'd been right, and I shoved it in my bag and headed back to the kitchen to say goodbye. He was leaning against the kitchen counter waiting for me, arms and legs crossed, eyes full of heat. I gave him a quick kiss and tried to keep walking, but his hand shot out and grabbed me around the waist, and he pulled me back to him.

His mouth brushed my neck with a kiss, and he spoke into my ear. "Have a good day, sweetheart. I think we need to discuss our future a bit more tonight. And then I think we really need to play with my toys."

Oh god.

I turned in his embrace. "When you say we need to discuss our future, you're not thinking of breaking up with me, are you?" I teased, knowing full well he had no plans for that. Not after last night.

"No. I'm thinking of getting us matching rings," he said in the kind of tone that told me he wasn't just thinking this, he was already planning it.

"You have the best thoughts, baby," I said with a smile, and he gave me one back.

And then he smacked me on the ass and said, "Okay, go. But be at my place by five. I've got plans for you."

"Yes, sir," I promised, loving the wild look his eyes got at my promise.

Ten minutes later, I was stuck in rush hour traffic. I should have felt stressed about it, but all I could bring myself to do was think of Kick. We sat bumper to bumper for what felt like ages, until, suddenly, there was a break in traffic and we all began moving at normal speed again.

Thank goodness.

I changed gears rapidly as I began to finally gain speed. My thoughts shifted from Kick to work and back to Kick again. I couldn't concentrate on anything but him for longer than a couple of minutes. This was going to be a long day.

And then it happened.

I never saw the car coming.

And I sure as hell never saw the truck coming.

I heard the screeches of tyres before I saw any of it.

All I saw after that were flashes of metal.

And then I saw darkness.

Chapter Eighteen

Kick

Fuck.

I pushed through the hospital doors, heart in my gut, and jogged the rest of the distance to the emergency room. It had been over half an hour since Loretta had phoned me to let me know Evie had been in a car accident.

Thirty fucking minutes too long.

My gut swirled with dread.

How fucking bad was this accident? Loretta hadn't been able to tell me much over the phone, and my mind had conjured up the worst possibilities.

As I entered the emergency room, Loretta rose from her seat and came to me, a look of sheer panic on her face.

Fuck.

Her arms reached out, and I pulled her close to hug her. "Kick . . . it's going to be bad . . . I just know it . . ." Her voice cracked, and she started crying.

I let her get it out and then asked, "Have you spoken to a doctor yet?"

Shaking her head, she said, "They haven't been able to tell me anything. No one's giving me anything!" Her voice gradually rose to almost a wail.

"Shhh," I whispered. Loretta wasn't the most stable woman and I could see she wasn't coping with this at all. "I'm going to go and see what I can find out. ·You wait here, okay?"

"Okay," she said, her voice barely audible.

I left her and approached one of the nurses at the counter. She gave me a bored 'what-the-fuck-do-you-want?' look. "I'm wanting information on my girlfriend. She was brought in after a car accident."

"Name?" Still with the bored look.

"Evie Bishop."

She typed Evie's name into her computer and after reading the screen for a moment, said, "Please take a seat. I'll call you as soon as you can go through and see her."

I did as she said and took a seat next to Loretta. Fuck knew how long we'd be waiting.

"Did they tell you anything?" she asked, her voice almost pleading for me to say yes.

I shook my head. "No, I think we're in for a long wait."

Thank fuck she was the kind of woman who didn't engage in unnecessary conversation. I didn't have the patience for that. Pulling my phone out, I said to her, "I'll be back in a minute." I stood and headed outside to ring King to let him know I wouldn't be back to the clubhouse any time soon.

"Kick," he answered, "I was just about to call you. We've heard rumours that your girlfriend's accident wasn't an accident."

"Keep talking," I said, more calmly than I felt. My blood was pumping furiously through my veins now.

"It seems this was a hit organised by Gambarro."

"Motherfucker!" I roared as I turned around and punched the brick wall behind me.

"I've got the boys finding out where Gambarro is. We think he's still out of the country but have to verify that. You stay with your woman, and we'll let you know once we have the info."

"Thanks, brother."

We ended the call and I stalked back inside.

Gambarro would fucking pay for this.

***

"Evie," I said softly, trying to wake her up. She'd been exhausted and had been drifting in and out of sleep for the last couple of hours while we'd been waiting for the all clear.

Her eyes fluttered open, then shut, and open again. She gave me a small smile before wincing and placing her hand to her side. Before she could speak, I placed my finger to her lips. "Shhh, baby, don't try to speak because it will probably hurt."

She had fractured some ribs in the accident. Besides that, she had whiplash but nothing else. She'd been lucky considering a car had rammed her, causing her to slide into the path of a truck. The good fortune of the day had been the quick thinking of the truck driver who had swerved to miss her, and, in doing so, had only clipped her car.

The doctors had done x-rays and verified it was only her ribs and that in time they would heal by themselves. They'd dosed her up on strong painkillers and had told me I could take her home soon.

Thank fuck.

She ignored my advice not to speak. "When can I go home?" she asked, her face contorting in pain with every word.

Loretta was standing on the other side of her bed and grabbed her hand. "They've said you can go home in the next hour or so. They've just got to get your discharge ready and your pain medication."

"Thanks, Mum." She hissed through the pain.

I frowned at her insistence to talk, and she just pulled a face

199

back at me. My woman was too damn stubborn sometimes.

The doctor came back to us with a smile. Looking at Evie, he announced, "You're good to go. The nurse will have your medication in a minute. If you experience any of those symptoms I mentioned to your family, you need to come straight back to the hospital." He waited for her response, and when she agreed, he nodded and left us alone.

I eyed her mum. "Can you give us a minute, Loretta?"

As she left, I raked my gaze over Evie again. Gambarro would hurt for this.

At her questioning look, I said, "Sweetheart, this wasn't an accident. This was retaliation for me getting your dad's debt wiped. The guy who organised this will pay, I promise you that." Her eyes widened, but before she could say something, I silenced her again with a finger to her lips. "I'm gonna take you home, and when I get the call from King, I'll organise for one of the boys to come over and watch out for you while I go and take care of this."

I watched as my words sunk in, not knowing how she would cope with that information, but needing to be upfront with her about it.

No more secrets.

She eventually nodded, and I let out a thankful breath.

Once I took care of this, we could all move forward.

***

I'd just settled Evie into her bed when I got the call from King. "Gambarro's flying into Sydney tonight. His driver is picking him up and taking him out to his country house. I'll round the boys up, and we'll meet him on the way to his house. Can you meet us at the clubhouse in about an hour?"

200

"Yeah, but can you send Nitro or Devil to watch over Evie? I don't want to leave her alone and chance one of his guys coming to finish off the job they started this morning."

"Good call, brother. I'll send Nitro," King promised and hung up.

Evie's gaze focused on me, and she gave me a questioning look. "Are you leaving now?"

Fuck, the pain I could hear in her voice made my stomach roll. To think I could have fucking lost her today. "Yeah, baby, I'll head out once Nitro arrives. He'll make sure you're okay."

Her hand reached for mine. "Thank you," she whispered.

"It's the least I can fuckin' do . . . for getting you into this mess."

"No, *I* got *you* into this mess, remember?" She gave me a small smile.

I nodded, and tried to lighten the mood. "Yeah, that's right, and it also means I won't get to play with you and my toys for awhile now."

She tried not to laugh, but couldn't quite help herself. However, the pain in her ribs stopped her, and her eyes welled up from the pain. "You and your fucking toys," she muttered, and a grin spread across my face.

I leant close to her face, and promised, "As soon as your pain eases, I'll be fucking you for days to make up for this."

"That's going to be a lot of days," she murmured.

"Yeah, I'm betting on it, sweetheart."

***

The dark road stretched out ahead of us, not a car in sight. The silence of the night blanketed us; the only sound to be heard was the rumble of our bikes. King had rounded ten of us up for

201

this job, but I'd made it clear back at the clubhouse that this was my gig. I would be the one to cause Gambarro's last breath.

His car was visible up ahead, and I gave the signal to hurry this shit along. We all picked up speed and a couple of minutes later we circled his car and forced it to pull over. I had no doubt Gambarro would be well protected, and I hoped like hell all of us left here in one piece tonight, but the other possibility was one all of us entertained when we participated in club business like this.

As the car came to a halt, we all trained our guns on it, waiting. It took a few minutes before one of the back doors opened and a gun was fired at us, narrowly missing King. He got pissed, and being the crazy asshole he was, he ran towards the car after dodging the bullets.

Fuck.

I couldn't let him go down for this, so I followed him. King reached the car first and he yanked the door open. As he did this, I covered him, and shot at the guy who lunged for King from the back seat. His body slumped out of the car and King shoved him out of the way. He pulled Gambarro out and pushed him hard up against the car.

"Well, hello there, motherfucker," he greeted him before turning to gesture at me, "I've got someone here who wants a word with you." He stepped out of the way and allowed me full access to Gambarro.

Adrenaline ran through my body, every nerve ending alive with the anticipation of bloodshed. I'd been surprised as fuck Gambarro didn't have more than one guy besides his driver with him. Devil had restrained the driver, and I was almost disappointed this had been so easy.

Gambarro's empty eyes flashed at me. "I see you got my message," he snarled.

"I got both your fuckin' messages, asshole," I snapped, my fingers itching to pull the trigger of the gun I had trained on him.

"I only sent one. I trust it got through to you."

I clubbed him with my gun. Not hard enough to knock him the fuck out, but just hard enough to cause him some pain. Pain he fucking deserved.

His head snapped back into place and blood ran down his face. "Have at it, asshole. You kill me, and you and your club won't know what the fuck hit you," he threatened.

"Fuck you!" I roared as I clubbed him again, this time a little harder, causing him to lose his balance and stumble. He didn't fall, though. When he straightened, I took in the blood now covering his face.

Fuck yeah.

"Kick, let's move this along," Hyde suggested. He was right; we needed to get this done and then get the hell out of here.

I lifted my gun and aimed it at his forehead. "The world will be a better place without you in it. I fuckin' hope you rot in hell."

My gun sounded, and Gambarro dropped. He hadn't even flinched at my words. So cold and dead on the inside, I bet he'd probably spent his life wondering each day if it would be his last. A lot of people would rejoice at the news of his death.

I stepped away from his body and turned to King. "Are we cleaning this up?"

He shook his head. "No."

His meaning was clear - this was a message, and we would let it speak for itself.

"Alright, boys, let's get the fuck out of here!" King yelled out, rounding everyone up. He jerked his chin at Devil. "Let the driver go. It's not his fault his boss was a prick." King never failed to surprise me; this kind of decision was rare.

With a deep sense of satisfaction, I headed home.

Killing someone like Gambarro rated highly on my 'I've-had-a-good-day-at-work' scale. I would never be convinced that ridding the earth of scum like him was a bad thing.

Especially not when my family was threatened.

Chapter Nineteen

Evie

Holy mother of God!

The pain shot through me as I tried to suck in a breath and shift in the bed. My eyes flew open and I stifled the cry trying to push through my lips.

"Baby, are you okay?" Kick's voice cut through my haze of pain.

I turned my head and found him standing next to the bed, his body bent at the waist, face hovering over mine. His distress at my agony warmed me, that he cared so much, but at the same time I hated to see him so worried. I tried to ease his mind. "I'm okay, but I need some painkillers, please."

He nodded and said, "Good. I'll be back in a minute."

I watched as he strode out of the room.

My man loved me.

Everything he did for me showed me just how deep that love was.

And I couldn't wait for him to get those matching rings.

When he came back, he had water and pills. Kneeling on the floor next to the bed, he asked, "Can you sit up?"

I shook my head, fearful of the pain that shifting would cause. I'd had hardly any sleep and I'd finally found a position that caused the least amount of pain; I didn't want to chance bringing more pain on.

"Okay, don't move," he said, as he passed me the painkillers.

"I'll hold the water for you."

I took the pills and he brought the glass of water to my lips and helped me swallow them. After he'd placed the glass on the bedside table, I gave him a small smile. "Thank you," I whispered.

He leant over and placed a kiss on my forehead. "I'm sorry." His words were simple, but I heard every last drop of pain and sorrow in them.

I gulped back the tears that threatened. Rapidly shaking my head, I said, "No, this isn't your fault, Kick. Don't you dare take that blame."

Kneeling again, his gaze grew serious, and my gut tightened, sensing where this conversation was headed. "You never need to worry about Gambarro again." His words were hard, and I knew from his tone and the way his entire body had tensed that he was worried about my reaction. He needed me to accept his actions.

"Good," I said, and watched as the worry eased out of his body. "And, baby, I will always feel that way about anything like this. I trust everything you do because I know it comes from a place of love and a need to protect those you love. Never doubt my love for you and belief in you."

He stared at me, and I saw the war waging in his soul. Kick was essentially a good person, but sometimes in life, things touched you and stained you in a way you could never recover from. They caused an irreversible shift in the way you saw the world around you, and in the way you dealt with the things that happened to you from that point on.

Sometimes, the path your journey veered on to led you to do things you'd never have considered previously.

And sometimes, in the hell you'd been delivered into, the end justified the means.

So I watched as he waged war, and I reached my hand up to lay gently against his cheek. "This is it, Kick. Can you feel it?"

He frowned. "Feel what?" he whispered, clearly confused at my obscure words.

"The moment where you know once and for all that there is nothing you could do that I wouldn't accept," I explained and waited for it to sink in.

"Fuck," he murmured, "I don't fuckin' deserve you."

"Yeah, you do," I said as I curled my hand around his neck and pulled his face to mine. He willingly gave me his lips and I kissed him with all the love and passion I felt for him. When we ended the kiss, I said, "Now, I do believe you have some rings to buy."

He grinned and raised a brow. "Oh, you think so, do you?"

It was my turn to raise a brow. "Questioning the woman who will be your wife one day soon is not a smart move."

Chuckling, he agreed. "You have me there, sweetheart. I learnt a long time ago that questioning the woman I love isn't a smart move."

"When was that?"

"I was seventeen at the time. It was the day I asked you to the senior dance, and you said no because I'd questioned a decision of yours to stand up for Joe Jensen the day before. You practically held me to ransom over that fuckin' dance, and in the end I had to backtrack on everything I'd said about that dickhead and pretend I fuckin' liked him to get you to agree to go with me."

I couldn't hide my surprise. "I thought you only asked me to that dance because you had no one else to go with."

His eyes turned soft. "No, baby, I asked you because I really wanted to take *you*. I wouldn't have become friends with fuckin' Joe Jensen if I didn't have to."

207

My ribs might have been in pure agony and my body and mind might have been exhausted, but this new knowledge buzzed through me, causing extreme happiness to settle in me.

Kick Hanson had loved me since he was seventeen, and he still loved me eighteen years later.

***

I slept for most of the day. Kick looked after me, staying close by all day. At four that afternoon, Mum and Julie came to visit. I'd been awake for about half an hour then so it turned out to be perfect timing.

"God, Evie, don't give us a scare like that again!" Julie said, her face a mask of worry. She'd brought flowers with her and arranged them in a vase I'd sent Kick to find. Placing the vase on the bedside table next to me, she bent and gave me an awkward kiss on my forehead. She still wasn't big on public displays of affection, and I figured a kiss was hard for her, but I appreciated the gesture, particularly seeing as though she couldn't hug me.

I smiled up at her. "I'll try not to," I promised, my glance shifting to catch Kick leaning against the door, arms folded over his chest and a contemplative look on his face. We held each other's gazes for a moment and then I gave mine back to Julie.

"Good," she said.

"The police said there were a few witnesses to the accident but none of them can remember the number plates of the car who caused it. One witness even said the car didn't have any. I don't think they're confident they can solve this," Mum told me, seemingly upset with this information.

"Well, I guess whoever it was will get theirs in the end; karma and all," I said, keen to change the topic of conversation.

208

"Have either of you heard from Dad lately?" I hadn't heard from him or seen him since the day he told me he didn't want Kick in my life.

Mum smiled, and that stunned me. She and Dad hadn't been close since he left after she cheated on him. "He and I have been in contact after he called and asked me to lunch the other week. Evie, he told me what you and Kick did for him and how awful he was to you about Kick. He regrets it, and he also regrets not following up on the counselling."

I wanted to believe everything she had said but after years of being let down by him, I struggled to buy it. "And?" I asked, my voice hard and guarding. I had to guard my heart from more disappointment.

Julie stepped in. "He's doing good with the counsellor . . . I've seen him a few times, and I'm proud of what he's doing."

My eyes widened.

Shit, if Julie was impressed, it meant Dad really *was* making progress.

"Okay, good," I said softly.

Mum looked hopeful as she asked the next question. "He wants to see you. Would you be up for that? He's worried about you."

Kick pushed off from the door he was leaning against and came towards me, concern etched on his face. "Is that a good idea?" he asked me.

I loved his concern, but I thought it might actually be good to see Dad. "It's alright, Kick, I want to see him. Maybe this will be the fresh start we all need."

As the afternoon progressed and we all loosened up with one another, I thought back to that conversation and hoped it really would be a fresh start for all of us.

An opportunity to put the pain of the last eighteen years

behind us once and for all.

Chapter Twenty

Kick

A few days later, King called Church. He'd put it off, giving me time to be with Evie, but he was right – we needed to take stock of where the club was at. I left Evie with her Mum and headed into the clubhouse.

Hyde greeted me with a slap on the back. "How's everything going, man?" he asked, his beef with me completely gone. *Jekyll and Hyde*.

"All good, but not holding out hope that Gambarro was bluffing the other night," I expressed my concern that Gambarro had indeed made plans for his crew to avenge his death if it ever were to happen.

His face darkened. "Yeah, I wouldn't put it past the motherfucker to have organised something."

We took our seats around the table and King began. "Has anyone heard anything from the Gambarro camp?" he asked, looking around the table. The resounding 'no' gave me only a tiny sliver of hope, and it appeared King thought the same way I did. "Well, keep your ears to ground and let me know the minute you hear something. We need to be prepared for this."

Everyone agreed to that, and then I raised my concern from the other night. "Gambarro said he'd only sent one message to us – the car accident. But my girlfriend's house was broken into the other night and trashed. Nothing was stolen. Now call me a paranoid bastard, but this feels odd. Have any of you had shit happen recently?"

I looked around the table and from the expressions on everyone's faces, I knew deep in my gut something was definitely odd with this. Nitro was the first to speak. "My sister's place was ransacked three nights ago."

Devil's vein in his neck twitched as he said, "Fuck, my brother was broken into a couple of nights ago."

Hyde was murderous. "Fuck!" he roared, standing. He looked like he was about to explode from his anger. "My sister owns a convenience store and it was held up two nights ago." His gaze zeroed in on King. "This is Silver Hell, isn't it? Those motherfuckers!"

If I thought Hyde was murderous, King was positively insane. He slammed his fist down on the table and looked around the table. "Those motherfucking cunts!" Giving his attention to Devil, he said, "I want you to look into this, you and Kick, and report back ASAP, yeah?"

Devil's eyes met mine, and we nodded. "Yeah, boss, will do," he agreed.

"Any other business to discuss?" King demanded, his wild eyes searching the room. When no one spoke up, the gavel came down and Church was done.

Fuck.

Shit just got real.

***

I gazed at Evie sitting in the bed. She'd progressed from lying down all the time to sitting for a while each day. I knew from experience how painful broken ribs were, and I also knew how long they took to recover from.

"What are you thinking?" she asked, keeping her eyes on

mine.

I smirked and pushed off from the wall to walk to the bed. Sitting next to her, I said, "I was thinking that my dick could shrivel up from lack of use over the next month or so."

"Really? Such deep thoughts you have, Kick," she said with a wink.

"That was your opportunity to tell me we could work without your pussy on this."

"Well, we could . . . you've always got two hands to take care of business," she responded, with a teasing gleam in her eye.

"Sweetheart, I'd much rather your hands sign up for this job."

She laughed and fuck if that didn't turn me the fuck on. Jesus, Evie only had to look at me these days and I was almost blowing a load. Her laugh didn't last long, though, because it caused her pain and she winced. But then she grew serious and asked, "Do you ever think we'll get to play with your toys?"

I shifted off the bed and threw my hands in the air. "Fuck, baby, you can't do that to a man when he's got no fuckin' hope of getting a hard-on taken care of."

"I'm sorry! I didn't mean to bring your toys up." She really did look apologetic, but that was no good to me once my dick was already hard.

I placed my finger to my lips. "Shhh, don't mention the toys again. At least not until you can fix *this* shit," I said, pointing to my hard cock.

Nodding, she opened her mouth to say something, but we were interrupted by a knock at the front door. I left her and went to answer the door. My brother and sister stood on the other side, surprising the hell out of me. Lina pushed past me before I could stop her, and asked, "Is Evie in her bedroom?"

213

I'd forgotten she knew this house; Evie and Lina had been close until the last time I broke up with Evie. "Yeah, just go on through," I muttered, knowing full well my sister wouldn't listen to me if I told her to wait.

Braden grinned at me as he took a step inside. "How are you, little brother?"

"Fuck, man, I'm tired. It's been a long week. And you?" I closed the door behind him.

"I'm good. Heard you had a blow up at Mum."

I raked my fingers through my hair. "Yeah, that woman . . ." my voice drifted off as thoughts of her cut through me. I wasn't sure I'd ever work my anger at her out of my system.

"I get it. I told her not to come around my place anymore, too," he admitted.

"Good. She doesn't deserve a place in our lives."

We'd made it to Evie's bedroom and she caught the last piece of our conversation. She looked up at me and asked, "Who doesn't deserve a place in your life?"

"Mum."

Lina piped up. "Oh, speaking of people who don't deserve a place in our lives . . . Dave has been given a transfer for work. He'll be leaving in a week."

I was concerned for her, and what this would mean but at the same time, I was over the fucking moon he wouldn't be around to harass her anymore. "Are you okay with that?" I asked, watching her closely for her real feelings on the matter.

Her face lit up with a smile. "Yes, because it gives us both space to move on, and it also gets him away from me and the kids when he's been drinking, which seems to be more often than not these days."

Evie reached for Lina's hand and gave it a squeeze. "That's great, Lina," she said with a smile.

214

"Yeah, thank fuck," I said, meaning every word of it.

For the first time in a long time, it felt like our families were healing and growing, and good shit was happening.

It had been a long time coming.

Chapter Twenty-One

Evie

Excitement bubbled through me at the fact I was finally getting to meet Kick's friends. As we walked into the clubhouse, I let my gaze roam over it, taking it all in. I'd imagined something similar, but not exactly the same. The non-descript brick building didn't scream biker to me, however the high fence surrounding the large building, and the obvious presence of security and a guy manning the front gate, did tell me something. The club took their security and protection seriously.

Once inside, I noted the dated paint on the walls, the worn carpet and the tired furniture. This clubhouse had seen better days, but I doubted the guys even saw it. The front door led down a long hall that was lined with framed photos of members. A quick glance told me some had passed, but mostly it appeared these photos were of current members. Once we were about halfway down the hallway, Kick turned left and walked through a wide doorway that led us into the bar area. And shit if I didn't get a surprise in there. This room had been freshened up, and it seemed to me it had been done by a woman. It had a lick of new cream paint, the carpet had been pulled up, and the cement floor had been polished. The lighting in this room was also different, brighter. Not to mention the furniture. New wood tables and chairs were scattered throughout, and today they were all occupied as bikers laughed and drank. My eyes narrowed on the couches. They were the only things in the room that did not look new, and by the quick glance I took, they didn't look like anything I would ever sit on.

Kick's arm came around my shoulder and he pulled me close. "You okay? Are your ribs giving you grief?"

Always looking out for me.

It had been a few weeks since the car accident and while I was still in a great deal of pain, I'd assured Kick I was up for today. A barbeque with the boys . . . no way was I turning that invitation down.

"This must be Evie!" a voice boomed from behind me.

Turning, I found a tall, built guy coming towards us. His dark hair hung down to his shoulders, and although it was messy looking, and he had a scar running down the left side of his face, and even though the glint in his eyes seemed crazy, I had to admit, this man was hot. Scary hot. Scary as in crazy, fucked-up, but hot nevertheless.

"Evie, King," Kick introduced us, and I gave King a huge smile. I didn't care if he came across as scary, he was the man who helped save battered women from their abusive husbands, and he was the man who helped Kick take care of the asshole who tried to kill me.

"Hi," I greeted him.

His eyes sparkled with mischief. "Fuck me, how the fuck did Kick score a woman as beautiful as you?"

"Fuck off," Kick said, and I practically felt the possessive vibes circle me.

Shit, my man's caveman side had kicked in.

And I kind of liked it.

King laughed, and Jesus, if that man was hot before, he was fucking sexy when he laughed and his eyes lit up.

Another guy entered the room and zeroed in on us. Shit,

another good-looking dude. This one had short dark hair and a beard. His arms were covered in tattoos and his brown eyes held a sadness to them. He smiled at me, but it was like his mouth was pretending because the smile sure as hell didn't hit his eyes.

Kick introduced him, "Nitro, this is Evie."

"Hi darlin'," he said, his voice deep and husky.

Good Lord, he would make some woman very happy one day. Kick had sent him over to look out for me once but he'd stayed outside so I hadn't gotten to lay eyes on him, and what a damn shame that was.

"Hi," I said, watching as his gaze on me changed from looking at me to pretty much looking through me. His eyes turned vacant, and I wondered where he went. My arms wanted to circle him in a hug and make it all better for him, whatever *it* was.

He excused himself to go and get a drink, but almost as soon as he'd left us, another two guys wandered in and came straight to us.

Huh . . . turned out Kick's friends were mostly all hot. Out of these two, I found one of them extremely attractive with his almost bald head, tattooed muscles and piercing blue eyes. It turned out his name was Devil, and I instantly liked him the minute Kick introduced us. The other guy scared the hell out of me. Sure, he was good looking, but I couldn't get past the hard, cold eyes that tracked my every movement, or the indifference I heard in his voice. It was like there was no feeling there, and as far as I was concerned, people who felt nothing were the scariest of them all.

"Hyde," he introduced himself.

"Evie," I replied, giving him a small smile. Even if he scared the shit out of me, I could still be polite to him. He surprised me with a smile back.

"Do you want a drink?" Kick asked.

I shook my head. "No, I don't want to chance it interfering with my painkillers."

"Shit, I forgot about that. Good call, babe," he said.

"You want a beer, Kick?" Devil asked.

"Yeah, thanks, brother," Kick replied, and Devil left to take care of it for him.

Hyde walked away, too, which left only me, King and Kick. King lowered his voice a little when he spoke. "The info you gave me on that drunk driver last week? I took care of him for you."

Kick stared at him and then nodded. I had no clue what they were referring to, but kept silent. If Kick wanted to fill me in, he would. And it turned out he did. He looked at me with a new sadness in his gaze that hadn't been there before. "The guy that killed Jeremy," he said softly, and I felt the pain in his words.

"Oh," I said, not sure what else to say, guessing that when King said he took care of him, he meant he *took care of him*.

King's face clouded over with anger. His gaze shifted between Kick and me when he said, "Assholes like that don't deserve to fucking live, sweetheart."

I sucked in a breath. He was right. "No, I don't suppose they do,' I murmured, holding his gaze.

He stared at me for a couple more moments, the angry mask still in place, and then he broke out in a grin and turned to Kick. "I like her," he declared, and then he left us to go and talk to the woman behind the bar.

I soaked in the atmosphere, looking around the bar at everyone having a good time. Without knowing these people, I could still sense the family vibe. Kick had spoken to me about his reasons for joining Storm, and the main reason was the family he found within the club. And I could grasp that now.

Devil came back to us, handing Kick his drink. Eyeing me, he said, "I hear you've agreed to marry this fucker."

I laughed and nodded. "Yes, not that he actually proposed to me."

"Bullshit," Kick said, "I proposed."

My eyes widened, and I placed a hand on my hip. "Oh, really? Was I asleep or knocked out from painkillers when you did it? Because I don't remember it," I challenged him.

Chuckling, he leant close to me, and let his lips brush mine before saying, "I suggested we should get matching rings. Do you seriously not remember that?"

I rolled my eyes. "Oh my god, Kick, that is *not* a proposal."

Devil interjected. "What would a proposal look like, sweetheart? Like, say, if Kick were to propose right now, what should he do?" There was a glint in his eyes that I couldn't pinpoint, but I decided to play along anyway.

"For a start, there'd be a really big, fucking ring. And then he'd get down on one knee and tell me how much he loves me and that he can't live without me. *And* he'd assure me that I was the only one for him and that we'd be together forever." I stopped and took a breath. They were both staring intently at me, and it unnerved me.

Devil raised his brows. "Anything else?"

I looked at Kick and shook my head. "No," I said softly. He was watching me with a strange look, almost as if he was soaking in everything I'd said and filing it away for later use.

And then Kick made my heart expand and find more space inside it to fill with love for him. With his eyes firmly on me, he reached his hand out to Devil who placed a box on his palm.

A ring box.

He took it and got down on one knee. Devil put his fingers in his mouth and whistled loudly to get everyone's attention. Kick looked up at me through eyes that were full of love. Taking my hand, he said, "Evie Bishop, I've loved you since I was a kid. I've never stopped loving you. And I never fuckin' will. I can't live without you, and I'm not just saying that. When I don't have you, I wander aimlessly; I have no purpose. But with you by my side, I belong, and I know what I'm doing. And as far as there being any other woman for me . . . no woman even comes close, never has, and never fuckin' will. I could be in a room of women and all I'd see would be you, and all I'd want would be you." He paused and pulled the ring from the box. It was a really fucking huge diamond ring. "Sweetheart, will you let me get us some matching rings? And then spend the rest of your life with me?"

Tears threatened to fall down my cheeks. I smiled through them, though, and nodded. "Yes," I whispered, and as he slid the ring on my finger, the room erupted with whistles and cheers, and lewd comments being yelled out at us. I was too damn happy to pay any attention to any of it. Instead, I threw my arms around Kick when he stood. I ignored the pain shooting out from my ribs. This wasn't an occasion to let a little bit of pain interfere with. "I love you, Kick Hanson," I said as his arms came around me.

He kissed me, and when he ended it, he said, "I love you, too, baby. And I've always known we'd be together forever. It just took us a little time to figure our shit out." He grinned and added, "You made me work for it, but I knew you still loved me, and that I'd eventually get you to relent."

"You're a sneaky bastard," I chastised him.

Grinning harder, he admitted, "Only where you're concerned. Anything for you, Evie Bishop."

I let the tears fall then.

Tears of happiness.

It had been a long, hard journey for us, but we'd eventually made it to where we were meant to be.

And I was so damn glad he'd made me relent.

Epilogue

Kick

I listened to the words coming out of Devil's mouth, and let him get them all out before I said anything. "It's been three months of bloodshed and loss, at *their* fuckin' insistence, and now they want to call a truce?" I flicked my gaze to King. "What the fuck do you think, Prez? 'Cause, for the record, I am against it. I say we bury those fuckers. And if you ask Nitro, he would say that, too."

King contemplated this new information regarding Silver Hell. I'd expected him to agree with me, but he threw me off when he didn't come straight out with it. Fuck, he'd experienced loss at their hands, too. Why the hell wasn't he saying *fuck yes, bury them*? Instead, he said, "Kick, it's your wedding day. Can we just get you the fuck through this and then make a decision?"

Devil seemed as stunned as I was. "I'm with Kick, I say bury them," he said.

A vein in King's neck ticked and he lost his loosely contained shit. "I say we don't fucking decide today!" he roared. "I just want one fucking day without those motherfuckers ruining it. Do you think we can have that?"

Jesus.

I shoved my fingers through my hair and then stretched my back and arms. Nodding at King, I agreed, "Yeah."

King huffed out a harsh breath and desperately tried to shake some of the tension out of his tightly wound body. "Good. Now let's get this wedding underway." He slapped me on the back as he pushed past me to head out of the clubhouse bar to the marquee we'd set up on the land we owned out the back of the clubhouse.

We watched him leave, and then Devil asked, "You ready for this, brother?"

I grinned. "More than fuckin' ready."

"You're a lucky asshole, to find a woman as good as Evie."

Fuck yeah.

"Kick!" We turned to see Lina rushing into the bar, looking stressed.

"What?" I asked, my own stress levels rising. Fuck, with all the shit we'd been through over the last three months, every little fucking thing stressed me.

"Evie's here. You need to get outside so you're waiting there when she walks in."

"For fuck's sake, Lina, don't do that. You had me worried something had happened to her or to someone else," I complained.

She pursed her lips. "Just get your ass out there."

I did as she said and walked out to the marquee to wait for Evie. I hadn't seen her since yesterday morning, and, fuck, I ached to see her. How the hell I'd gone three years without her, I had no clue, because these days, being away from her a mere twenty-four hours was hell.

I'd asked Braden to be my best man, and he leant next to me now and said, "Never thought I'd see the day."

"What?" I asked, not taking my eyes off where Evie would enter.

"The day my brother got married."

Something in his voice caused me to turn and face him. He

was emotional about this. "Yeah, me either," I admitted, "but thank fuck she came back to me."

"Who would have thought, all those years ago when you two were kids, that you'd end up married one day?"

I wasn't the kind of person to look back too often in life. My motto was to keep going forwards, but Braden was a sentimental bastard. Instead of replying to him, I simply nodded in agreement.

"You know," he mused, "it's sad, but I think in a way Shelly's death brought you two together."

My eyebrows drew together. "How the fuck do you figure that?" Jesus, what a morbid fucking thought.

"No, think about it. After her death and all the shit our families went through with our parents cheating, and then all the shit Evie went through, she needed you, and, in a weird way, you needed her. It brought you closer."

"I still don't follow," I muttered.

"You do realise Evie blamed herself for Shelly's death, right?"

Fuck.

"No, I didn't know that," I said softly.

"Jesus, Kick, you really were ignorant, weren't you? When Shelly fell out of the tree, Evie was supposed to be watching her, but she was too busy flirting with you. She blames herself because of that, I'm sure of it. And on top of the blame she dumped on herself, she ended up doubting herself after being bullied. *You* helped her and gave her the confidence in herself she needed. In return, she ended up loving you unconditionally, and gave you the sense of family you didn't get from ours."

I stared at him. "Well fuck, Braden, what are you? Some kind of psych?" I was fucking impressed with analysis, though.

He grinned. "Fuck off." He tapped his head and said, "I'm

225

just the brains of the family, asshole."

A hush came over the marquee, and I turned to see Evie entering. Fuck, my wife-to-be was beautiful. She had on a fitted white long dress that made her tits pop just enough for me but not so much that every fucking asshole here would be ogling them. And she had her hair up, which I loved because it gave me full access to her neck.

As she walked towards me, our eyes did not leave each other. I was so captivated by her gaze, I couldn't even drag mine down her body to check out her killer curves. Over the past few months, Evie had stopped worrying so much about her weight and dieting and all that bullshit. And I was fucking rejoicing because her curves had returned.

She's made me a happy man in more ways than one.

When she came closer, her father, who had walked her down the aisle, gave me her hand, and I did my best not to snatch it. Fuck, I had it bad today.

Once I held her hand in mine, I pulled her to me and whispered, "Fuck, baby, you look beautiful."

She blessed me with a smile that could take a man's breath away. "Thank you."

She really had nothing to be thanking me for because *I* was the one who should be thanking *her*.

Evie had brought peace to my life.

Bonus Chapter

Evie

After he'd unlocked the front door of our home, Kick scooped me up into his arms. "Welcome home, Mrs Hanson," he said with a huge grin on his face.

Mrs Hanson.

I grinned back at him, my tummy still full of the butterflies that had inhabited it all day. My wedding day truly had been the best day of my life. "I love you, Mr Hanson," I said softly.

Kick entered the house, closed the door behind him with his boot, and walked intently down the hall. My body buzzed with desire. It had been a long day and I was exhausted, but never too exhausted to play with Kick.

As he walked down the hall, my gaze landed on the frames we'd hung. Photos of us and of our family lined the walls. I remembered the day we'd hung them. Kick had announced his desire to fill the walls with photos of our children. He wanted three and couldn't wait to get started. I'd gone off birth control immediately and he'd spent every morning and night since working on making it happen.

I had good news for him tonight, but first, I would let him play because I feared once he was told, he would overprotective, and pull back on the rough play.

When we reached our bedroom at the end of the hall, he entered it and dumped me on the bed. I bounced a little and then rested on my elbows, watching him, waiting for his next move.

His intense gaze roamed over my body as he removed his cut and placed it on the armchair in the corner of the room. I loved that armchair. It was where he often sat and watched me while I slept. Waking up to find Kick's hungry eyes on me was the best way to wake up.

He slowly removed the rest of his clothes, and my desire built as he drew it out.

I was impatient for my man.

When he crawled onto the bed, over me, I thought I would burst from the desire. "Kick-"

"Shhh," he whispered, placing his finger over my lips to silence me. He pushed me onto my back and then bent to take one of my nipples into his mouth.

Yes.

I gripped the sheet and dug my toes into the bed. I'd been without Kick's mouth for over twenty-four hours. This was like coming home.

He let my nipple go and raised his head to look at me, his need raw on his face. "You got any idea just how ready I am to fuck you?" he growled as he pressed his erection into me.

Fuck.

I reached my hands to grab the back of his head and pulled his face to mine. Our lips collided a second later in a rough kiss; the kiss we'd both been aching for all day. While he kissed me, he began tearing at my clothes. My wedding dress was practically sewn onto me, though, and he quickly grew impatient and frustrated with its removal.

Pulling his lips from mine, he complained, "Fuck, Evie, are you trying to block my access tonight?" His gaze moved over my dress and I could see his mind trying to figure out the best way to get it off.

I pushed him off me and moved off the bed. Turning around to show him the back of the dress, I said, "You've got some buttons to undo, and don't even think of ripping it off. This dress cost me a fortune." The buttons ran the length of the dress and Maree had warned me Kick would get frustrated with it, but I'd loved it too much to worry about that. Plus, I figured by the time he got me out of it, he'd be so worked up that I'd be guaranteed some rough sex.

He came to me and began working on the buttons. When he was about half way down my back, he said, "Jesus fuck, woman, I was a fan of this dress until now."

I grinned to myself. Smiling sweetly at him, I said, "Sorry, baby, I thought you'd like it more."

He practically growled and his touch grew rougher as his fingers worked harder and faster to get the buttons undone. A couple of minutes later, he had the dress and my underwear off and he spun me around to face him. I sucked in a breath at his face. I'd never seen him so desperate to have me. And I felt that desperation deep inside.

I reached out to take hold of his cock, but he grabbed it before I got there. "I think I'm gonna have to cuff you tonight, sweetheart," he said, his breathing growing ragged. He let my hand go. "Wait there," he commanded and walked to the drawer where he kept his toys.

After rummaging through the drawer for what felt like ages, he shoved it closed, and muttered, "Fuck." Looking over at me, he asked, "Do you remember where the fuck I put the cuffs?"

Shaking my head, I said, "No."

Without saying anything else, he stalked out of the room. I did as he said and stayed where I was, hoping he would hurry back.

A minute later, he stalked back into the bedroom, no cuffs in sight. I sensed his frustration and when he grabbed something from the drawer and slammed it shut, I heard that frustration. Kick was not a patient man.

He came to me, holding the roll of bondage tape he didn't use that often. Cuffs were his preference, or rope. But tape was quick to use and I figured that was why he'd gone with it tonight. His eyes met mine, and he said, "On the bed, baby, back against the headboard, arms up."

Our bed had a padded headboard, which he'd insisted on for my comfort. Attached to the wall just above the headboard was a wrought iron bar and that was one of Kick's favourite things in our entire house. It was what he often used to restrain me. The bar was also one of my favourite things because when he used it, I was guaranteed the best orgasms.

I sat on the bed, watching with anticipation as he came to me. He grabbed one of my hands and taped it to the bar, and then repeated this with my other hand. My core clenched; he was rougher than I'd hoped for, and I loved it.

He dumped the tape on the floor and then took hold of my jaw with one hand while the other one trailed down my neck to my breasts. His eyes followed his hand and lingered on my chest for a while before coming back to meet my gaze. "Fucking hell, Evie, even after all these years, I want you so damn much." He brought his lips to mine and kissed me while still holding my jaw firmly. I could feel his need in his kiss, and my heart beat faster in my chest at the thought of what was to come.

After he ended the kiss, he let me go and spread my legs wide, bringing my knees up so my feet were resting on the bed. His eyes focused on my pussy, and I watched as he fought to control himself. Kick was good at making himself wait, but that didn't mean his restraint was easy to achieve. He had to work hard at it.

Shifting onto his stomach, he positioned his mouth so he could lick the length of my pussy. I shut my eyes and let the pleasure consume me. His hands gripped my legs, and his lips and tongue brought me to orgasm faster than they ever had. I screamed out his name and fought against the tape that was restraining me.

I need to touch him.

"Don't fight it, baby," he whispered as he moved and brought his face to mine.

I opened my eyes and stared into his. Oh god, I loved this man. "Undo me, Kick, I want to touch you . . ."

I hadn't expected him to listen to me, but he moved off the bed, grabbed his knife from the drawer and came back to free me. However, he didn't have plans for me to touch him. He grabbed hold of me and pulled me to him. Then he moved a pillow down the bed and flipped me so my belly was lying over the pillow with my ass slightly raised. He took hold of both my hands and stretched my arms out on the bed above me while he lay over the top of me. Pressing my hands into the bed, he grunted as he slammed his cock into me.

Hard.

Rough.

Yes.

He pulled out and thrust back in. "Fuck," he growled against my ear sending even more pleasure through me. I loved hearing his need escape from his lips.

The room was silent around us except for the feral sounds of Kick fucking me. Bodies slamming together, breaths coming hard and fast, grunts as we both reached for our release, and, finally, the roar as we orgasmed.

Kick collapsed on top of me and I didn't even care that his weight was almost crushing me. I was lost in the pleasure he'd just given me. Eventually, he did move off me to lie next to me. He pulled me against his body, positioning me so my head was resting on his chest.

We were silent for a few minutes until he said, "Promise me we'll still be fucking like that when we're sixty."

I laughed and lifted my head to look up at him. "If I know you as well as I think I know you, we'll still be fucking like that when we're ninety."

Grinning at me, he nodded. "I reckon you might be right there, sweetheart."

I moved so I was sitting next to him. My fingers traced a lazy pattern on his chest and my eyes met his. Smiling, I whispered, "I can only see one thing slowing us down."

He frowned. "What?"

"The kids we're going to have."

He sat up, the look on his face changing. Staring at me with a look of amazement, he asked, "Are you about to tell me what I think you're about to tell me?"

I nodded, a wash of emotion taking over me. "Yes. You're going to be a daddy."

His eyes widened and a huge grin filled his face. And then he practically crushed me to the bed and kissed me. He kissed me for an eternity, and when he'd finished, he looked down at me through eyes that couldn't hide his love even if he tried, and said, "I love you, Evie Hanson."

I looped my arms around his neck, and said, "Not as much as I love you, Kick Hanson."

He chuckled. "You might think you wear the pants in this relationship, sweetheart, but I'm telling you now, if we have a daughter, I'm the boss of her. And that's a 'we clear' statement."

I laughed. "Oh God, I hope we have a girl. Kick Hanson

232

scaring off boys . . . I want to watch that."

He groaned, a look of pure pain flashing across his face. "Fuck, that's gonna be worse than dealing with men watching you."

As I watched my man declare his love for me in more ways than one, I realised how happy I was.

Finally.

We'd been through so much and we'd fought so hard for this over the years. And we'd finally done it. We'd created our own family, and this family would always love and protect its own.

Always.

Acknowledgements

Relent was originally written for the Black Hearts Anthology (that never went ahead). I met some amazing women while we worked on that anthology, and I'd like to thank them for their friendship, support and advice. Crystal Spears, JC Emery, River Savage, Ryan Michele, MN Forgy, AC Bextor & Emily Minton – thank you girls, and although we were all disappointed it never went ahead, I am so grateful for the opportunity to get to know you.

I always need to thank my family and friends for their support. Without them giving me the space to do my thing, my books would never make to release. I love you all.

I really need to send huge thanks to my editor, Karen. You put up with my inability to meet editing deadlines and I am so thankful for all the work you do for me.

To my beautiful cover designer, Letitia Hasser from Romantic Book Affair Designs – this cover is the bomb! Thank you so much for nailing it!

My amazing PA, Melanie. Thank you so much baaaaabe! I would be lost without you.

To my STORMCHASERS – I love you girls!! Thank you for all your wonderful support and for the friendships we have made. I hope to get to meet you at one of the signing events I'll be at this year.

To my gorgeous readers. Thank you so much for buying my books and reading them. And for loving my characters as much as you do. It blows me away every damn day xx

About The Author

Dreamer.
Coffee Lover.
Gypsy at heart.
Bad boy addict.

USA Today Bestselling Aussie author who writes about alpha men & the women they love.

When I'm not creating with words you will find me either creating with paper, paint & ink, exploring the world or curled up with a good book and chocolate.

I love Keith Urban, Maroon 5, Pink, Florida Georgia Line, Bon Jovi, Matchbox 20, Lady Antebellum and pretty much any singer/band that is country or rock.

I'm addicted to Scandal, Suits, Nashville, The Good Wife & wish that they would create a never-ending season of Sons of Anarchy.

I'm thankful to have found amazing readers who share my alpha addiction and love my story writing style. I'm also thankful that many of these readers have become friends. The best thing in the world is finding your tribe.

www.ninalevinebooks.com

Made in the USA
Middletown, DE
22 November 2019